I0618500

THE BOX

Also by Deanna Madden

Helena Landless

Gaslight and Fog

The Haunted Garden (a novella)

The Wall

Forbidden Places

The World Beyond: A Novel of Ancient Greece

THE BOX

DEANNA MADDEN

FLYING DUTCHMAN PRESS

Copyright © 2018 Deanna Madden

All rights reserved.

ISBN-10: 0692185917
ISBN-13: 978-0692185919

Cover design by SelfPubBookCovers.com/Shardel

Flying Dutchman Press

2018

This is a work of fiction. Names, characters, places, and incidents
either are the product of the author's imagination or are used
fictitiously. Any resemblance to actual persons, living or dead, events,
or locales is entirely coincidental.

for my mother and father
with love

The universe is a pretty big place. If it's just us, [it] seems like an awful waste of space.

—Carl Sagan, *Contact*

Sedona, Arizona, 1999

B en had traveled to Sedona to view the eclipse. It was not a total eclipse but close to it. He had never been to Sedona before and was excited to have a chance to explore the area with its unique rock formations. He rented a Jeep and spent the day before the eclipse driving on backroads and hiking some of the trails. He had just bought a new camera and was using it to capture shots of the scenic red rocks for which the region was known.

He didn't believe in the so-called vortexes and mystical nonsense associated with the area. For him it was enough that it was a place of phenomenal natural beauty and about as unlike the rich foliage and waterfalls of Upstate New York, where he had grown up, as it could be. It was a matter of luck that the eclipse was happening during his summer break. In two weeks he would be back in the classroom teaching restless undergrads the basics of astronomy. He must make the most of this opportunity while he could.

He had already hiked two trails when he spotted a trail on

the map that led to a cave. Ever since he was a boy, he had loved caves. If there was a cave here, he had to check it out.

There were other hikers coming out of the cave when he arrived forty-five minutes later. He stopped to talk to them for a few minutes. It was like they were all fellow travelers. That was one of the things he liked about hiking—the sense of camaraderie. It was like they were all part of a grand enterprise.

The cave had a large mouth but soon narrowed to a tight passageway. Fortunately he had a flashlight with him. He'd been a Boy Scout when he was young, and basic survival precautions were ingrained in him. He was a little embarrassed by these at times, but they had held him in good stead on more than one occasion, so he saw no reason to jettison them now.

He was glad he had thought to bring a flashlight. He would have been walking in pitch blackness otherwise. When the cave opened into a large cavern, he could shine his flashlight at the ceiling and walls to get a better idea of the space he found himself in. Two hikers passing by, who had been shouting a few minutes before to hear their voices echo, told him the vortex was up ahead. He thanked them and kept going, grateful for the silence that followed in their wake.

After that the cave narrowed again. Then he turned a corner and found himself unexpectedly in sunlight, facing a gap that looked out on sandstone cliffs and a hot blue sky. Incredible. It was as if the cave wall had been blown away. He could see for miles. Lifting his camera, he snapped a shot.

He was so taken by the view that it was a moment before he noticed the girl.

She was staring at the panorama as if she had never seen anything like it. One hand was touching the wall, as if she needed to brace herself to keep her balance. She looked to be in her early twenties. Suddenly he worried that she might try to jump. He thought he ought to move closer, speak to her.

"Hey, there," he said and took a tentative step toward her.

She turned her head with a look of confusion. He hadn't meant to startle her.

"Are you alone?" He took another step. Maybe that had been the wrong thing to say. She might think he was trying to make a move on her. It did seem odd that she was alone. Had she gotten separated from a friend?

"It's okay," he said, holding up his hands so she could see they were empty except for the flashlight. "I'm Ben."

Still she stood there with that look on her face, like a deer caught in the headlights of an oncoming car.

"What's your name?" he asked.

She stared at him. She still looked as if she might jump— or turn and run.

Maybe she didn't speak English. Maybe she had gotten separated from her tour group.

"My name is Ben," he said and patted his chest. "Ben."

She smiled, uncertain. "Kath-leen," she said, the words barely more than a whisper with an odd break in the middle.

At least he was making progress. Apparently she understood English.

"Kathleen what?" he asked, but she stared blankly at him. Maybe she had a learning disability, he told himself. She looked normal, but her reactions were a bit strange.

"Where are you from?" he asked, trying a new tack.

She looked out at the view dreamily. Could she be high on something?

He wanted to get her attention away from that ledge with its deadly drop off. "I'm from Upstate New York. Where are you from?" He didn't care if he sounded like an idiot, as long as it helped to distract her.

"Here," she said. "Right here."

"Sedona?"

She didn't answer. Now she was frowning thoughtfully at something by her feet. A metal box of some sort. She nudged it with her foot.

"I'm here for the eclipse," he said. If he kept talking, that might keep her mind off jumping—if that's what she was contemplating.

She looked at him and smiled. The light from the opening struck her face and his heart melted.

She no longer looked as if she might jump. Why had he thought that?

"It's so beautiful," she said, looking out at the view again. "Have you ever seen anything so beautiful?" She had a slight accent, but he couldn't place it.

"Are you lost?" he asked. "I mean, do you know your way back?" As near as he could tell, she had no flashlight. Not unless it was in that box by her feet.

"No, not lost," she said.

"I have a flashlight," he said. "If you want, you could walk back with me."

She was still looking out at the view, as if reluctant to leave it.

"Maybe your friends are waiting for you outside," he suggested.

"Yes," she said in a vague and noncommittal way.

Had she really hiked in alone with no flashlight? Was there no one wondering where she was?

She reached down and retrieved the box. It caught the light and reflected it like a mirror. Aluminum maybe? A curious item to bring into a cave. And she had no backpack.

Maybe she had fallen down and bumped her head before he had come upon her. That would explain why she seemed disoriented.

"Tell me about the eclipse you came to see," she said, her voice stronger now, more sure of herself.

He was surprised she had picked up on that. "It's a near total eclipse from here," he said. "I'm going to take photos of it."

She smiled. "The sun or the moon?"

Evidently she hadn't seen it in the news. "A solar eclipse. Tomorrow at noon."

"May I watch it with you?" she asked.

His heart almost stopped. "Yes. Of course. I mean, that would be great."

A few minutes later she shyly took his arm as they crossed the cavern with the high ceiling. He hoped she didn't have family or friends or a tour group waiting for her when they stepped out of the cave. His imagination rushed ahead, envisioning a dinner together at one of Sedona's open-air cafes. Nothing like this had ever happened to him before. He wished he could prolong these last minutes they had together before they reached the mouth of the cave and he would have to go his way and she would go hers. He didn't want their time together to end. Had she meant it when she said she wanted to watch the eclipse with him?

When they reached the narrow passage, he held her hand, inching ahead with the flashlight lighting their way. He wished he could think of something clever to say so she wouldn't forget him. He only had this little bit of time, and then he might never see her again. He didn't even know her last name.

Then the walls fell back. A few more steps and light was flooding in the mouth of the cave, where other hikers were preparing to enter.

They blinked as they stepped out into the sunlight. Again he was struck by something about her that he couldn't quite put his finger on as the sunlight fell on her. The box gleamed where she cradled it against her body. He looked around, half expecting someone to rush up to her and say, "Oh, here you are!" but no one did.

"What now?" she asked, looking around at the stony landscape as if seeing it for the first time and then looking at him as if he had the answer.

"Do you need a ride?" he asked.

"A ride?"

"I have a Jeep."

She tilted her head, considering.

"I can take you home," he suggested.

"Home?" She frowned slightly.

His heart thudded. Maybe she wasn't from here after all. Maybe he had misunderstood. Suppose she had bumped her head while she was in the cave and she had amnesia or a concussion or something. Maybe he ought to drive her to a hospital or a police station.

"Look," she said and pointed to the red rock formations looming behind them.

At that moment he decided to stop fretting about who she was. Something wonderful had just happened to him in that cave. He had met Kathleen, and whoever she was, he instinctively knew she was very special. If she needed a friend, he would be that friend. He didn't have much time before he had to return to his life in New York, but he would change his flight if he could and stay a little longer in Sedona, just so he could spend some time with her before he had to leave.

"Wait," he said. "I want to take a photograph. Of us."

If he lost her, he would at least have the photograph to remind him of her. He set up his tripod to take a timed photo. She kept smiling, as if she found his camera amusing, or maybe it was him she found amusing. He didn't care. Her hair was tousled. She was laughing now. She had set the box behind them on a rock. He took his place beside her, his arm around her waist, and waited for the click of the shutter.

CHAPTER 1

It was a heart attack they said. His housekeeper found him slumped over in his chair when she let herself in. My mind kept going back to that. I should have been there. He should not have been alone when it happened.

Now I sat surrounded by his friends and colleagues, listening to a minister extoll his kindness and how he would be missed. It all seemed unreal. I just wanted the funeral to be over so I could be alone. They meant well—these people who had come to pay their respects—but I could hardly bear sitting through it. None of them would miss my grandfather the way I would.

When the eulogy was over, I still had to shake hands and listen to all the well-intentioned comments and expressions of sympathy. I just wanted to run out the door, climb into my car, and cry.

"If you need anything, just let me know," said Mrs. Calhoun, patting my arm. She worked in the office in the astronomy department at the university. Her hair was greyer than when I last saw her, and her face had a few more lines.

"He was a wonderful man," said an elderly gent leaning on a cane. "You should be very proud of him." His face was familiar, but I couldn't recall his name. I had met him once at a fundraiser.

Then Mr. Malinsky, who had taught with my grandfather at the university and was a close friend of his, pressed a key in my hand and closed my fingers around it. His eyes were moist as he looked into mine. "He wanted you to have this, Lauren. He told me if anything should happen to him, to give this to you." His hand felt paper-thin and trembled a little as he held mine. He was nearly as old as my grandfather but still teaching at the university.

I looked down at the key. "What is it?"

"It's for a safe deposit box at the bank."

"I don't understand."

"He said to be sure I gave this to you myself. He was very specific."

I dropped the key into my purse. I didn't want to think about money. I assumed it was money. What else did one put in a safe deposit box? But what did money matter now? All the money in the world would not bring my grandfather back.

We stepped out into the sunlight then, but my ordeal wasn't over. Next came the solemn procession of cars to the cemetery and more hard moments to stumble through as well as I could at the gravesite, all in a blur of tears, until I felt numb.

Afterward I drove to my grandfather's apartment building. I told myself I shouldn't. It would be too painful. I should wait a few days. But the urge to go there was overwhelming. I wanted to take refuge in those familiar rooms surrounded by his books and possessions. I wanted to curl up inside myself like a sea creature in its shell. Besides, sooner or later I would have to sort through his possessions. I might as well get started.

For the past ten years my grandfather had lived in an old brown brick apartment building in a rundown neighborhood getting more rundown every year. After I had moved out the year before when I enrolled at the university, I had tried to persuade him to move too, but he had dismissed my concerns about the neighborhood, preferring to stay where he was. He said he was too old to be uprooted. Nowhere else would feel like home.

I parked my car in a guest stall in the parking lot and used a key card to access the building. It was hard to believe he wouldn't be sitting there in his apartment as usual in his leather armchair reading a book. I hesitated before using my key on the door. But I was here now, so why not go in? Taking a deep breath, I slid the key card into its slot, heard the small click of the lock release, and pushed the door open.

The sight that met my eyes made me gasp. Papers littered the floor. Books had been pulled from the bookcase and dropped haphazardly on the floor. A small wastebasket was overturned, spilling its contents on the carpet. As I stared at the room in shock, a chill ran through me. Somebody had broken in. I glanced uneasily at the two doors that led to the bedrooms, wondering if the intruder was still in the apartment. But it was so quiet I felt certain that whoever had done this was long gone. I pulled out my phone and punched in the number for the building manager. He answered at the third ring.

"Yes, yes. I already reported it," he said. "A tenant down the hall found the door open yesterday. Didn't you get the message I left on your voicemail?"

I hadn't felt like checking my voicemail over the past twenty-four hours. Too many condolence calls. I had turned off my phone.

"Was anything stolen?" I asked.

"You tell me. We just left it the way we found it. I locked it back up. You'll have to let me know if anything was stolen— although I doubt there's anything that can be done about it. No one saw anything."

I felt angry when I hung up. Of course, it wasn't his fault the place had been broken into and ransacked. But I felt outraged that someone would try to steal from a harmless old man who had just died. How could people be so callous? No doubt someone had read his obituary in the newspaper and thought his apartment might be easy pickings. I looked around, heartbroken. Had they taken anything of importance?

My grandfather wasn't a rich man. You could see that at a glance. What did he have that anyone would want? Who would do such a thing? Drug addicts? Teens? Petty thieves looking for cash or meds or something they could sell?

I felt like crying. But I had already shed too many tears, and crying wouldn't accomplish anything. I had a job to do.

I began by collecting the scattered pages of his manuscript and arranging them in a neat stack on his desk. For the past year he had been working on a book, *A Guide to the Stars*. Now it would never be finished. I supposed I would have to throw away his half-finished manuscript. The thought made me feel sad. All the hours of work he had put into it! I wondered if one of his friends at the university might want to finish it. But I doubted it. They had their own projects to work on. Why would they want to finish a book that a retired professor had been putting together and that was only a layman's guide to the stars, not a scientific treatise that broke new ground? They would see it as a waste of time.

My grandfather, who had been an astronomy professor for forty years, had taught me the names of stars and constellations when I was growing up. He gave me my first telescope when I was ten. He had hoped I would choose to study astronomy, but my discovery of the violin soon after had pushed all thoughts of astronomy out of my head. From that point on I only wanted to be a violinist. If he was disappointed, he hid it, and in the years that followed he lined up violin lessons and faithfully showed up for all my recitals, my biggest champion.

Once I had picked up the papers and books and righted the wastebasket, I surveyed the room again. So what was missing? What would a thief have been looking for? Money? I opened a drawer of his desk. The contents were messy, but they always had been, hadn't they? My grandfather had seldom spent time organizing the contents of drawers. I couldn't tell if someone had rifled through them or not. My eyes moved to the small TV sitting on a squat table in the corner of the room. The thief hadn't bothered to take it, but then it was old and probably not worth anything. Doubtless for the same reason my grandfather's computer was still sitting on his desk. It was too out-of-date to tempt a thief. Was it possible a thief had found nothing of value to steal?

I sighed and walked into my grandfather's bedroom. The

closet door stood open and his clothes were pushed carelessly aside as if the intruder had rummaged about looking for something. The drawers of the bureau had been dumped on the bed. Socks and underwear lay strewn across the faded brown bedspread. There was no point in putting underwear back in drawers. I would have to bag my grandfather's clothes to give to Goodwill. I looked around the room. What was there to keep? My glance fell on a framed photo sitting on the bureau of the two of us taken on my seventeenth birthday. He had set the timer and snapped it as we sat smiling behind my birthday cake, the little candles burning. A lump formed in my throat at the thought that I would never celebrate another birthday with him. I reached for the photo. Behind it was one of my mother and father. They were smiling into the camera as if they hadn't a care in the world. How young they looked! I ran my finger across the glass.

My mother had been only twenty-five when she died of a pulmonary embolism following childbirth. My birth. She had been teaching music courses at the university after giving up a promising career as a violinist when she married my father, who was teaching in the astronomy department. My father had helped her get a job teaching music appreciation classes to undergrads and giving violin lessons. The fact that she had played the violin was probably why I had felt drawn to the instrument myself. It was a way for me to connect to the mother I never knew.

My father had died in a car accident when I was five. I barely remembered him. After that I had lived with my grandparents. My grandmother died of cancer when I was nine, and then it was just me and my grandfather. Now he was gone and it was just me.

I laid the photos on the bed, found a plastic bag in the kitchen, and began to collect my grandfather's clothes and stow them in the bag. When it was half-filled, I looked about and saw how much there was still to do. Shirts lay crumpled on the floor of the closet. Shirts he would never wear again. Suddenly I didn't feel like doing more. The rest would have to wait.

But before I left, I wanted to take a peek into my old room. I had left little behind when I moved out. This room too had been ransacked. The stuffed green dragon I had left on my bed was still there, but the drawers of my dresser had been pulled out and emptied on the bed. The closet door stood open, and clothes had been pulled from hangers and tossed carelessly on the floor, just like in my grandfather's bedroom. It was so senseless. I reached down and picked up a small purple-haired troll and set it back on the nightstand, where it grinned at me. Too bad it couldn't tell me what had happened.

If an intruder had taken anything, I didn't know what. And I hadn't the heart to keep sifting through my grandfather's things and mementos of the past. I would come back another day when I felt more up to the task. I retrieved the two framed photos from my grandfather's bedroom. Then I let myself out of the apartment and drove back to the old white three-story house on University Drive where I rented rooms on the first floor.

I had my own side entry, a feature which had been the deciding factor in renting the rooms. Well, that and the fact that they were close to the university and cheap. I was fitting my key in the lock when I realized the door wasn't locked. That was strange. Was it possible I had been so distracted when I left to go to the funeral that I had neglected to lock it? I felt uneasy as I pushed the door open. My stomach dropped at the scene of devastation that met my eyes. It was even worse than my grandfather's apartment. Sofa pillows had been ripped open, a lamp knocked over and broken, and my poster of planets against a starry backdrop—a gift from my grandfather on my fifteenth birthday—ripped from the wall.

I felt a rush of anger. Why had someone done this? I had nothing of value for anyone to steal. On second thought, maybe I did. I ran to my bedroom, my heart in my mouth. Clothes were scattered on the bed and the floor. I searched frantically among the heap of clothes and shoes on the closet floor until I found my violin. It had been dumped from its case, but it didn't appear to be damaged, thank god! I felt a wave of relief as I clutched it to my chest. It wasn't a rare violin, but I couldn't have borne to part with it. I knew how to coax sounds from it that I doubted I would be able to coax from another violin, at least not one I could afford. It frightened me to think how close I may have come to losing it.

I couldn't believe my apartment had been broken into. First my grandfather's and now mine. And on the same day as his funeral. Talk about having a bad day! I pulled out my phone, sighed, and called 911.

CHAPTER 2

There were two of them when they showed up twenty minutes later, an older bald cop who asked the questions and a younger cop who looked about the room and didn't say much. Clearly the older cop was in charge.

"Was anything taken?" he asked.

"I don't know," I told him. "I just got home and found it like this."

He nodded and glanced into my bedroom. I had left it the way I had found it. That's what I was supposed to do, right? So why did I feel embarrassed for them to see it like that?

"I just got home from my grandfather's funeral," I explained.

"Do you know anyone who might have done this?"

"No, of course not. The really strange thing is my grandfather's apartment on Clinton was also broken into."

"Did you report that?"

"No, but his building manager did."

He looked around the room again. I couldn't tell what he was thinking. He looked bored. Probably he saw apartments

16

and houses that had been broken into all the time. Mine was nothing special.

"Matt, you done?" he called to the younger cop, who was dusting the doorknob for fingerprints. Or at least that's what he appeared to be doing.

"Yeah, almost."

I had a sinking feeling they weren't going to do anything about it. For them this was just routine. They came, they looked, they took notes and left. It was just a job for them, not the traumatic event that it was for me.

"Neighbors see anything?" the bald cop asked me.

"I don't know." Did he think I had run out to ask them if they had? Wasn't that *their* job?

"Guess we're done here then."

Through the open door I watched him saunter back to his patrol car parked at the curb. The sky was overcast and it looked as if it would soon rain. Apparently he wasn't going to ask my neighbors if they saw anything. Apparently that would be up to me. What had been the point of calling them?

"Your lock is busted," the young cop said. He was still standing by the door.

"Great."

"You probably shouldn't stay here tonight until you get it fixed."

I could tie rope around it or something, couldn't I? I didn't really feel like finding someplace else to stay. Definitely I wasn't going to sleep at my grandfather's. I just wanted to be alone in my apartment to grieve for him and put everything back where it belonged.

"You have someone you can stay with?" he asked as if he had read my mind. Maybe he had run into young women reluctant to abandon their apartments before. I made an effort to be polite.

"I suppose so."

"You a college student?"

I looked down at the pile of textbooks by my feet. Not hard to guess that. Well, at least the thief hadn't stolen any books. I had my violin and my books. I supposed I should be grateful.

"Don't mind Steve. He's always like that." He was apologizing for his partner.

I looked at him more closely. He was about my age, curly black hair, warm brown eyes, a friendly smile, and he was trying to make me feel better. He fumbled at his shirt pocket, plucked out a small card, and handed it to me.

"What's this?"

He looked embarrassed. "My card. In case you need to report something else. Like if you find something is missing."

Officer Matthew Malone, I read. "Thanks."

"It's my first week on the job."

I nodded. That explained his awkwardness and shyness. A rookie cop.

"Sorry about your grandfather," he said.

That made two of us.

After they left, I barricaded the door as well as I could with two dining chairs because I didn't want to leave my apartment despite what the rookie cop had said. Later I slept on the sofa because it was nearer the door in case someone tried to break in. I have no idea what I thought I could do to stop an intruder, but I had my phone next to me in case I needed to call 911 during the night. Fortunately, that didn't prove to be necessary.

The locksmith arrived in the morning while I was drinking coffee and checking my messages.

I felt better now that I had had time to clean up the mess left by my intruder. Or intru*ders*. There may have been more than one. The coffee helped too. Both break-ins seemed less upsetting now. I could think about my grandfather instead. If he were still alive, I would have told him this was proof he should move to a better neighborhood or at least a building with better security.

Of course, it was different in my case. I was a struggling college student. I couldn't afford a more expensive apartment. But then it hit me that maybe that was no longer true since whatever my grandfather had left behind was now mine. Or soon would be once the paperwork and legalities were over. I doubted it was much. He had never been interested in amassing wealth. Material possessions weren't important to him. Like my father, he only wanted to be able to study the stars.

Remembering, I felt a lump in my throat and tears sprang to my eyes again. It was hard to believe he was gone. Of course, I had always known someday he would die and I would be left alone. But I had hoped that day was still faraway. At least I could comfort myself with the thought that he had spent his life the way he wanted. How many people could say that?

I knew he wouldn't have wanted me to sit about crying. I could have skipped classes, but I thought keeping busy would make me feel better. I could throw myself into my studies and not give myself time to brood.

In the evening I had orchestra practice. I had been lucky to get a place in the local orchestra. We practiced every Monday night. I looked forward to these sessions, and tonight was no exception since it would help take my mind off my grandfather. Besides, it because it was our last rehearsal before Wednesday's concert.

I arrived early and felt relieved to lose myself in the hour-and-a-half rehearsal. For a while I didn't have to think about anything except the notes I played on my violin and the way the sounds of our instruments melded together. Afterward I felt it had been a needed break from all I had been going through.

I was putting my violin back in its case when I noticed a folded newspaper someone had left behind on a chair. What caught my eye was a photo of Mr. Malinsky, my grandfather's friend who had given me the key at his funeral. I wondered why there was a picture of him in the paper. Curious, I unfolded it. A headline caught my eye. *Astronomy Professor Murdered.* I stared at the words. How was this possible? I had just seen him yesterday at the funeral.

I would have liked to read the article then and there, but everyone around me was leaving and a security guard was getting ready to turn out the lights, so I pulled on my jacket and tucked the newspaper under my arm, intending to read it later.

"Hey, sorry about your grandfather," said a clarinetist. His name was Dave and he had a wife and two kids. I had been to their house once for a party.

"Thanks," I said and forced a smile. I picked up my violin case and headed for the door.

As I drove home in the rain, I thought about the article. How could Mr. Malinsky be dead? I remembered how he had pressed the key into my hand at my grandfather's funeral. If only I had taken the time to talk to him! I hadn't even thanked him. He must have thought I was ungrateful. And now I would never have the chance to apologize.

I recognized Matthew Malone's voice at once when he answered his phone. Although I hadn't heard him speak a dozen words, his voice seemed familiar. I felt a little jolt of pleasure, which was silly because I didn't know him.

I gathered my courage and launched in. "You said I should call you if anything came up."

"That's right."

"I saw in the newspaper that a friend of my grandfather's was murdered—Joseph Malinsky."

There was silence at the other end. I plunged on before I lost my nerve. "Can you tell me how he died?"

He hesitated. "Sorry, no. Did you find anything missing?" His voice was brisk, business-like.

"No, but I'd really like to know how he died." He probably thought I was just being nosy. Maybe I was.

"Look, I can't talk to you right now," he said. "Can I call you back?"

I listened to the flat buzz of the dial tone after he hung up and felt disappointed. What had I expected? I looked at the grainy newspaper photo of Mr. Malinsky again. It hardly looked like him. Did his death have anything to do with my grandfather? That thought had nudged its way into my mind half a dozen times now. Of course it didn't, I told myself. It was just a coincidence. I had to stop obsessing about his death. I had even dreamed about him last night. In my dream I saw him across a crowded room, but before I could get to him, he disappeared. Odd that I had dreamed about him and not my grandfather.

I slipped my phone into my purse. There was no time to wait for Matthew Malone to call me back. If I didn't leave now, I would be late for my first class.

Not until my morning classes were over did I have a chance to check my messages. I felt a small rush of adrenaline when I saw Matthew Malone had texted me.

Meet me at Mama Mia's at seven. —Matt.

Was he asking me on a date? Really? Wasn't that sort of weird? For all he knew I had a boyfriend. For all *I* knew *he* had a girlfriend. On the other hand, maybe it wasn't a date. Maybe he thought Mama Mia's was a neutral space in which to meet. But why not just tell me over the phone how Mr. Malinsky had died? That would be simple enough. I didn't want to have a date with someone I didn't know. I was tempted to text him back: *Thank you but no.* But then I might never know how Mr. Malinsky had died. I bit my lip and stared at the text. Oh, it was just dinner. What was I fretting about? I could meet him this once and then never see him again. Before I changed my mind, I texted back *ok* and hoped I wouldn't regret it later.

CHAPTER 3

I ought to have my head examined, I told myself as I climbed out of my car that evening in the parking lot a block from Mama Mia's. I had changed my clothes three times before deciding on a black shirt and black pants. Being a musician, I had lots of black. I knew it was ridiculous to worry about how I looked. In fact, it was ridiculous to be there at all. Really, I should just get back in my car and drive home again. I could say something had come up. Or that the timing was bad, which it was. I shouldn't be going on a date so soon after losing my grandfather. If only I could ask my grandfather for advice. Of course, he would say he trusted my judgment. He always said that. But I wasn't sure *I* did. What should I do? Giving up when I was only a block away seemed cowardly. Besides, didn't I owe it to my grandfather to find out what had happened to Mr. Malinsky? Mr. Malinsky had been his friend. This was the least I could do.

As I stood there debating with myself, I felt raindrops strike my bare arm. *Oh great. Rain. Just what I didn't need.*

Sighing, I shouldered my purse and sprinted toward the restaurant. Thank god I had opted for flats. Inside it was crowded and noisy. I glanced around nervously and didn't spot Matthew Malone. The dimly lit room was packed with customers sitting at tables covered with red tablecloths. Candles glowed in amber glass holders on every table. I had been there before, but I didn't remember it being quite so overwhelming. Maybe that was because it hadn't involved a date with a stranger. I felt the urge to turn and run, but a hostess was smiling expectantly at me. She was a pretty redhead with lavender eyeshadow and black nail polish who barely looked out of high school.

"I'm supposed to meet someone," I told her, my eyes roving again across the room.

Then I saw him waving from a small table by the window that fronted the street. I excused myself from the waitress and walked toward him, making my way among the tables, feeling self-conscious. Too late to back out now.

"I wasn't sure you'd come," he said as I slid onto the chair across from him.

"Why not?"

"The weather." He glanced toward the window next to us.

He looked different than I'd remembered, probably because he wasn't wearing his uniform now. Instead he wore a white shirt and had a large watch with a leather band strapped on his wrist. That didn't make me feel any less nervous as I looked at him across the flickering candle. He smiled. Was it my imagination or was he nervous too?

A waitress handed me a menu. I felt him watching me as I looked it over. I could hardly hear myself think over the buzz of voices, clatter of dishes and cutlery, and piped music in the background. How was this a good place to talk? Outside the window people rushed by on the pavement, heads down, and cars sped by in the street. It was raining harder now. Umbrellas had sprouted. I regretted having left mine in my car.

"Do you come here often?" I asked, trying to break the ice.

He grinned. "You mean, do I bring girls here often? Not really. My brother works in the kitchen."

What did that mean? He didn't bring girls here *because* his brother worked in the kitchen or were the two unrelated?

I tried again. "You live around here?"

"On Franklin."

I studied the menu, ordered a salad, and tried to relax.

"You got any brothers or sisters?" he asked. "Or is it just you?" He was trying to break the ice too.

"Just me."

"I come from a big family."

"I've always envied people with large families." Did he realize almost no one was an only child? Growing up, I had been asked more times than I could remember why I didn't have any brothers or sisters. I had never managed to come up with a good answer.

"It's got its drawbacks," he said.

"Like what?"

He squinted slightly as he thought and then enumerated them on his fingers. "Lack of privacy. A room you have to share. Hand-me-down clothes. Waiting your turn to use the bathroom. Someone to tell you off when you get too full of yourself. Especially that last one."

"Sounds good to me." I glanced around the room. Crowded places made me nervous. It was a mistake to have come. What was I doing there?

"What do you study at the university?" he asked, casting about for a new topic. "No, let me guess. An art major, right?" He grinned.

"Music."

He lifted his arms as if celebrating having guessed correctly, which he hadn't. "What kind of music?"

"Classical. I play the violin."

"No kidding?" He looked impressed.

I couldn't play this game. I should never have come. I only wanted to know what happened to Mr. Malinsky. Maybe I should just ask.

"Matthew—"

"Call me Matt."

"Matt. About Mr. Malinsky . . ."

"Yeah. Did you know him well?"

Did I know him well? I thought about that. He used to give me pennies when I was a kid and he came to visit my grandfather. I always thought of him as almost an uncle. He was a widower, like my grandfather, and had no children. But, no, I hadn't known him *well*.

"He was my grandfather's friend. They played checkers. Look, I thought you were going to tell me how he died."

"How he died? Maybe I gave you the wrong idea. It's an ongoing investigation."

A small basket of rolls arrived just then, interrupting us. After the waitress walked away, I picked up my knife, preparing to butter a roll, and then laid it down again. I could just leave, I told myself.

"When did you last see Joseph Malinsky?" he asked.

"At my grandfather's funeral on Sunday."

"It was later that night when he was killed."

Had he invited me here to interrogate me about Mr. Malinsky? Was that what this was about? I had thought I had come to question him, but had he in fact set up this meeting to question *me*? Had I totally misunderstood?

He didn't appear to notice my sudden reticence.

"Did he seem like anything was bothering him?"

So maybe he *was* interrogating me. Why not answer his questions? It wasn't like I had anything to hide.

"I only talked to him for a minute. He gave me a key."

"A key?"

"Yes, a key to a safe deposit box. Something my grandfather left for me." I threw a furtive glance toward the door. It looked so far away—all those tables and people between us and the door.

"Why did he have that?" Matt gazed at me steadily.

Again I noticed he had nice eyes. I looked away, determined not to be distracted. "Because my grandfather gave it to him. Because my grandfather trusted him. I don't know."

"Did you look in this safe deposit box?"

"No, not yet. Anyway it's probably just money. I don't really feel like rushing over to the bank and . . ."

"I doubt it's money."

I met those warm brown eyes again. "Why? What else would it be?"

"People generally put money in an account or a trust, not in a safe deposit box."

"What then?"

"Papers . . . important papers, like deeds or birth certificates. Or jewelry."

I shook my head. "He never cared about property or jewelry . . . not unless . . ."

"Not unless what?"

I hesitated. I didn't know Matt. Could I trust him? "Not unless it belonged to my father. Or mother."

He waited.

"My mother died when I was born. My father when I was five."

"No brothers or sisters. No parents, no grandfather. Please tell me you've got someone somewhere. A boyfriend maybe?"

I had to smile. He was so much better at this than I was. Very adroit how he had slipped that in. "No boyfriend. I do have a great-aunt in Florida."

Our food arrived at that moment, saving me from further embarrassment. After the waitress left, he forked a bite of linguine into his mouth and paused to chew it. "A great-aunt. That's good."

I felt myself flush. "I'm not Little Orphan Annie. I can take care of myself."

"I'm sure you can. I never meant to suggest otherwise."

He had managed to find out if I had a boyfriend or not. I had found out nothing that I had come to find out.

"So you're not going to tell me how Mr. Malinsky died?" I asked, poking my fork about in my salad. I should have told them to hold the black olives.

He sighed and touched his napkin to his lips. Did I mention he had nice lips?

"His throat was cut with a knife."

I stared at him, shocked. I'm not sure what I had expected but something less violent. Poor Mr. Malinsky! Who would do such a thing? And why? If someone wanted to rob him, it wouldn't have been that hard. He was just a helpless old man. They didn't have to kill him.

"His place was pretty well trashed. Whoever killed him was looking for something. Whether they found it or not, we don't know. Might have been addicts. There are so many out there now, hopped up on heroin or crack or meth. Opioids too. You can't imagine how much there is of that."

"I could never do a job like yours."

We looked at each other across the table—in our own little bubble of space in this crowded, noisy room.

"I could never play a violin."

"It just takes a lot of practice."

He grinned. "Sure."

No doubt about it, he was a good-looking guy—those puppy-dog brown eyes, curly black hair, and the killer smile. But he was a policeman. I was studying to be a violinist. We had nothing in common. We came from totally different worlds. If my apartment had not been broken into, we would never have met.

"Thank you for telling me about Mr. Malinsky," I said.

"Thanks for showing up."

"You could have just told me on the phone."

He shrugged. "But this was nice, wasn't it?" He had a dimple when he smiled. It vanished as he turned serious. "You did get that lock fixed, didn't you?"

"Yes." I rolled my eyes.

"Good. Look, you think maybe we could get together again sometime?"

Was he asking me out on *another* date? I should say no. I didn't know him. Not really. Maybe he was dangerous. No, he wasn't dangerous. Actually he was very sweet. But what would be the point? We were too different.

"How about tomorrow night?" he asked, unfazed by my lack of enthusiastic response. "We could take in a movie or something."

I realized I had the perfect reason to turn him down.

"Sorry. I can't. I have a concert." I tried to sound contrite.

"I could come and watch you play your violin."

His smile twitched. Suddenly it seemed mean to refuse. Really what would it hurt if he came and sat in the audience and watched? In fact, maybe it would be the easiest way to discourage him. He would be bored and realize we had nothing in common.

By the time the meal was over I had told him where the concert would be and when. In return he insisted on walking me to my car. It had stopped raining and the wet pavement gleamed under the streetlights. The air had that ozone-charged smell that made it seem as if the world had been washed clean. As I reached for the car handle, he reached too and his hand caught mine. Our lips met a second later. I hadn't meant for that to happen. It just did. We stood like that for a long minute, kissing. For once the voice in my head that usually pointed out all the reasons I should not be doing this fell silent.

"Mmm," he said when we finally broke apart.

I felt as if something had shifted between us, but I wasn't sure if that was a good thing. My head was spinning and I felt a little breathless. I reached again for the car door handle, determined to make my escape. "I should go now. So I'll see you tomorrow?"

"You will definitely see me tomorrow."

CHAPTER 4

It was disconcerting to find myself thinking about Matt as I sat through classes the next day. I didn't want the thought of him to keep distracting me from the lecture on Baroque music, but it did. I considered texting him and telling him not to come to the concert, but what possible excuse could I give for changing my mind?

After class I went to the library to check out some books on Prokofiev for a term paper I was working on. I grabbed a late lunch at the Campus Corner and tried not to think about Matt. What had possessed me to agree he could come to the concert? What had possessed him to want to? He probably felt more at home with Garth Brooks or Taylor Swift than Vivaldi.

I stopped by my grandfather's apartment after my last class and tried to make some progress on sorting through his belongings, but being there made me feel depressed. It was too quiet, too deserted. Everywhere I looked, I was reminded of him. The sight of his bifocals lying forlornly on the kitchen counter brought me to the verge of tears. The pile of manuscript pages stacked on his desk made a lump rise in my throat. After twenty minutes of opening and closing cupboard doors without accomplishing much of anything, I gave up, drove home, showered, and ate a tuna sandwich. I always got jitters before a concert. I knew they would go away once it was underway.

Because the concert was scheduled on a weekday, the auditorium was only half full. After taking my seat on the stage, I looked around nervously to see if Matt was there. When I didn't see him, I thought maybe he had decided not to come after all. Oddly this made me feel a little disappointed. Had I really been hoping he would come?

"Sorry about your grandfather," the violinist next to me said. Sheila was pregnant and just starting to show, although it was hardly noticeable in the black dress she was wearing. With her long blonde hair she looked as composed and elegant as ever.

"Thanks," I said and proceeded to tune my violin. Maybe it wasn't disappointment about Matt I was feeling. After all, I hardly knew him. Maybe it was just the sadness of losing my grandfather. Matt was right. I did feel alone. Who did I have now that my grandfather was gone? No one.

Stop that, I scolded myself. *You are not going to start feeling sorry for yourself. He would not have wanted you to.*

"I lost my mom last year," Sheila said, tucking a strand of long blonde hair behind her ear. "Breast cancer. It was horrible." She grimaced.

"I'm sorry," I said.

"Yeah, me too. She never got to see her grandkid. It sucks."

Focus, I told myself, listening to the instruments tune up around me. I opened my sheet music and tucked my violin under my chin. It was important to put everything else out of my mind and concentrate. Mr. Hajek's voice echoed in my head. *Nothing else matters.* How many times had I heard him say that during my violin lessons? Once the concert started I must think of nothing else. Not my grandfather. Not Matt. Only the music.

I glanced again at the audience. That was when I saw him hurrying down the aisle and making his way to a seat midway back. So he had come after all.

After the concert he was waiting for me near the door. My heart beat faster when I saw him. He broke into a grin. There was that dimple again.

"That was great," he said.

"You weren't bored?"

"Nah."

"Have you been to a concert before?"

He pretended to think hard about this. "Do rock concerts count?"

I laughed.

"You got me."

"It wasn't your kind of music."

"Give me a chance."

"Country and Western, right?"

He pretended to think hard about this question too. "I'm more a Bruno Mars kind of guy."

I laughed again. I couldn't help it.

"You've got to cut me some slack here," he said. "Hey, you want to go somewhere? Get a drink or a cup of coffee?"

I glanced at my car, not sure it was safe to leave it there. I also wasn't sure I should go somewhere with him. But if he had been willing to sit through the concert, shouldn't I be willing to go with him for a drink or a cup of coffee?

"It'll be okay till we get back," he assured me. "Come on."

I stowed my violin case in the trunk of my car, hoping he was right, then walked with him to a faded white Chevy with a bumper sticker that said *Beam Me Up*.

Before we got in, he threw his head back to look up at the night sky. "Have you ever seen so many stars?"

The October air was crisp, and I could clearly make out Cassiopeia, Andromeda, and Pegasus.

"There's one that's moving," he said, pointing. "Maybe it's a UFO."

"That's a plane," I told him.

"Are you sure? How about that one over there?" He pointed again, this time to a bright pinpoint of light near the horizon.

"The International Space Station."

"No kidding? Are you making that up? I bet you're making that up."

"Can I show you something?" I asked on impulse.

"Absolutely. What do you want to show me?"

"You'll see."

We climbed in his car and I directed him where to go. Ten minutes later we arrived at the observatory on the north part of campus. Except for a few other cars the parking area was empty.

"What are we going to do—break in?" he asked as we got out. "You do remember I'm a cop, right?"

"Trust me."

"Oh, trust you? Really? That's supposed to be my line."

When I pushed the door of the observatory open, a white-haired security guard sitting at the front desk looked up. He smiled when he saw me.

"Lauren," he said. "Haven't seen you around here for a while. Sorry to hear about your granddad."

"Thanks, Howard," I said. "Okay if we go up to the observation deck?"

"Sure. You'll have it to yourselves."

I signed us in on his clipboard.

"This is very mysterious," Matt said in a low voice as we stepped into the elevator.

I pushed the button for the observation deck.

"Don't tell me you're going to show me the big telescope," he said as we rode up.

"No, it's booked in advance, and you have to get approval. We're just going to use one of the smaller telescopes."

When the elevator stopped, we stepped out onto a deck open to the sky where there were seven mounted telescopes gleaming under the light of a crescent moon. I chose the nearest and looked through it.

"Look, you can see Rigel."

I stepped aside and he tried it.

"Which one is it?"

"The brightest one. Above it you can see three stars together. That's Orion's Belt."

He looked up at the sky and then back through the telescope. "Yeah, I see it. How do you know this stuff?"

"My grandfather was an astronomer. He used to teach here at the university."

He looked at me and his lip twitched. "No kidding—your grandfather was a professor here?"

"Yes. My dad too."

"Your dad too? Mine's a plumber."

"So? He probably makes as much as mine did."

Matt laughed. "Maybe so." He put his arm around me. "Where was that star again?"

I showed him.

He kissed me then. I shivered. Had I been waiting for him to do that again?

"Hey, look," he said. "A shooting star. That's supposed to be good luck, isn't it?"

"I think you're supposed to make a wish on it," I said, a little breathless.

"I think I just did."

CHAPTER 5

I wasn't quite sure how it had happened. Certainly I hadn't intended for it to happen. After taking me back to my car, Matt insisted on following me to see that I got home safely. I told myself on the way back to my apartment not to invite him in, but then I weakened at the last minute—another of those kisses that took my breath away and left me in a daze—and after that there was no turning back.

Now we were lying in my bed with his arm around me. I felt as if I had just surfaced from being underwater. My head had not cleared yet.

"So what got you interested in the violin?" he asked.

"I think it was because my mother played the violin. It was a way to feel closer to her. How about you? What made you decide to be a cop?"

"Well, I had to do something and I didn't want to be a plumber. Toilets, leaky faucets, backed up pipes." He grimaced. "I don't know. Maybe I watched too many cop shows when I was a kid. How could being a plumber compete with that?"

"So you like being a cop?"

"Yeah, most of the time. Hey, I'm the new guy on the block. Ask me after somebody starts shooting at me."

"You aren't worried about that?"

"We all have to take chances."

"Is your mother okay with that?"

"You know how mothers are . . . Oh, sorry. I wasn't thinking."

"It's all right. I never knew her."

"But still . . ."

"She's like this huge black hole in my life. You wouldn't think you would miss someone you never knew . . ."

"But you do."

"Yeah, I do."

He kissed the top of my head. "I'm sure your mom would be very proud of you."

"You know, when I'm playing my violin—like in the concert tonight—sometimes I feel like she's there, you know, in the audience listening."

"Maybe she is."

"You must think I'm crazy."

"I think you're just about the sexiest girl I've ever met. Not to mention the only violinist and the only one who can point out Rigel."

"And the International Space Station."

"That too."

"Matt—"

"No, don't say it. You have that look in your eyes again."

"What look?"

"That look of doubt. Just give me a chance. That's all I ask." He glanced at his watch. "And now, much as I hate to, I have to go. If I want to stay on the force, I have to report for duty bright and early tomorrow morning."

As he pulled on his shirt, he bumped the nightstand.

"Whoops." He stooped to pick up something that had fallen on the rug. "What's this?"

I saw something small in his hand gleam dully in the light from the window. "Oh, that's the key Mr. Malinsky gave me. The one I told you about."

He turned it thoughtfully in his fingers. "You checked it out yet?"

"No."

"Not the least bit curious?"

Well, maybe I was. I should at least see what was in the safe deposit box, right? So after my classes finished the next day, I went to my grandfather's bank with the key and a copy of his death certificate. The death certificate turned out to be unnecessary. My grandfather had included my name on the box. All I had to do was show my I.D.

A trim middle-aged woman wearing a white blouse, dark suit, and heels led me to a small room with a table and a few minutes later brought the box to me. It was larger than I expected. I wondered what could be in it. After she left, I put the key into the lock, took a deep breath, and opened it. Matt had been right. There was no money in it, although there were some bonds. The main object was an aluminum box about nine inches tall—at least I thought it was aluminum, although it seemed more iridescent than aluminum and had an almost translucent quality. Taped to the top was an envelope with my name scrawled on it in black ink in flowing but shaky letters. I recognized my grandfather's handwriting. Carefully I tore open the envelope. Inside was a folded letter from my grandfather dated a year ago.

Dear Lauren,

If you are reading this, it means I'm gone. Maybe I should have told you about this box a long time ago, but I wanted to wait until you were grown. The truth is I don't fully understand what it is myself. I just know it may be dangerous. I was tempted to destroy it, but I'm not sure how to do that— at least not without taking a risk I'm not willing to take. And I wasn't sure I had the right. You see, this box belonged to your mother. According to Ben, she put great store by it, but she also said no one must ever open it. She didn't say why, but Ben got the impression that something bad would happen. Who knows, maybe she was just superstitious. She never did tell him where she got the box. He figured when she was ready she would, but then she died. Now we'll never know why she didn't want anyone to open it. I'm passing it on to you as part of your legacy from your mother. It's one of the few things I have of hers to pass on to you.

The truth is she was a mysterious woman, and not until she died did we realize how little we knew about her. Ben knew nothing about the family she came from. She told him she grew up in California, but she was vague about where, and when he suggested they go visit, she said she wasn't interested. The past was past. She had no desire to go back to it. Ben assumed she had bad memories, but he didn't really know.

So now the box belongs to you, and you will have to decide what to do with it. Because she was so insistent that it should not be opened, I suggest you err on the side of caution and NOT open it. Leaving it in a safe deposit box or other container in a secure location is probably a good idea.

Please know that I love you very much and regret that I couldn't be there longer for you, but I have every confidence in the fine young woman you are becoming.
Love, Grandpa

I read the letter over several times, wishing he had told me about the box while he was still alive. I had so many questions. What made the box dangerous? Maybe my mother had said that to keep my father from looking in it. Maybe it held secrets from her past. But even if that were true, what could it possibly contain that might be *dangerous*? Was there information in it that she considered dangerous? Or was there something literally dangerous in the box—like anthrax spores or a bomb? Surely not. If it had truly been dangerous, why keep it?

I examined the box more closely. The lid could not simply be lifted off. It was sealed with a wide band of transparent tape. Below the tape the box was subtly decorated with tiny markings that almost looked like words but not in any language or alphabet I recognized. These markings were so fine as to be unnoticeable unless you held the box up to a light and looked at it closely.

So what should I do? I wondered. Should I leave the mystery box locked away in a safe deposit box as my grandfather suggested? Somehow it seemed a shame to hide it away in a bank vault. It looked like it belonged in a museum, displayed where people could see it. On the other hand, what if it *was* dangerous? I turned it in my hands. It looked harmless enough. And the thought that it might contain clues about my mother's past tantalized me. Why not take it home with me? I could always bring it back later and lock it away if I decided not to open it. Right?

When I exited the room, the woman in the white blouse and dark suit was standing outside the door. She looked at me in surprise, her eyes flying to the box in my hands, but she pressed her lips together and said nothing, merely nodded, then stepped into the room I had just vacated.

I half expected someone to challenge me as I crossed the gleaming tile floor headed toward the glass entrance doors, but no one did. I walked out of the bank carrying the box. Outside in the sunlight, it looked different. Not really like aluminum. Maybe an alloy of some sort. There was a pearlescent quality about it that reminded me of an abalone shell. A man I passed glanced at it oddly. Suddenly I felt conspicuous. I wished I could hide the box, but it was too large to fit in my shoulder bag. I tried to ignore the curious stares I received and breathed a sigh of relief when I reached my car in the parking garage. My fingers were trembling as I placed the box on the seat beside me and turned the key in the ignition.

As I pulled out onto the street, I tried to shake the sense of unease I felt. Why should I feel so uneasy? I had every right to take the box. It was mine after all. I glanced at it sitting there on the seat beside me. Had I made a mistake by taking it with me? *This is silly*, I told myself. *It's just a box.* I glanced in my rearview mirror. Had that white SUV been behind me when I pulled out of the parking garage? What did it matter if it had? No one cared that I had walked out of the bank with the box. It was of no consequence to anyone but me. Unless, of course, it was valuable. Or what was in it was. And then only if someone *knew*. I regretted now that I hadn't concealed it when I had walked out of the bank. I should have asked for a bag of some sort to put it in. Why hadn't I thought of that? Well, too late now.

I tried to tell myself that it was just a coincidence that the white SUV was still behind me as I neared University Drive. But that didn't stop me from growing more alarmed. I told myself if the SUV followed me when I turned onto University, I would know for sure it was tailing me. What would I do then? Drive past the house? Park and lock my car doors? Call 911 on my cell? What did people do in situations like this? But the SUV didn't turn when I turned. It kept going. I felt immensely relieved as I pulled up to the curb. All the same I broke into a run as I carried the box to the house.

Once inside, I set it in the middle of my small kitchen table, where it seemed to catch the sunlight from the window. I could see it out of the corner of my eye as I moved about the kitchen cutting up a salad for lunch. So should I open it or not? I wanted to know what was in it, but my grandfather's warning kept running through my mind. Suppose he was right? Suppose it was dangerous. He had been concerned enough to keep the box locked away in a bank vault all these years.

I glanced at my watch as I finished my salad. Twelve forty-five. Time to go. I grabbed my book, shoulder bag, and violin case and dashed for my car. It was hard not to think about the box while I was driving. The classical music station on my car radio failed to push it out of my mind. And later the lecture by Professor Thompson on Handel didn't keep my thoughts from straying to it. After class I found an open practice room and finally was able to forget about the box as I swept my bow across the strings of my violin and lost myself in a Brahms concerto.

I sometimes wondered if this was how my mother had felt when she was playing. Everything else fell away. This was all that mattered. I was always happiest when I was playing my violin. I would close my eyes and let the music carry me to that special place where I felt I truly belonged. I had my first glimpse of that place when I was ten and received my first lesson on the violin from Mrs. Anderson, a sweet old lady with the patience of a saint who when she was young had played with the New York Philharmonic. My grandfather thought maybe my desire to be a violinist was just a phase I would outgrow, but I had known even then that this was what I was meant to do. The sound of a violin awakened something deep within me and spoke to me as nothing else did.

When I emerged from the music building, I felt uneasy again— as if someone were watching me. I looked around nervously as I headed for my car but saw only other students crossing the quad, and none of them were paying any attention to me. The feeling persisted even when I was in my car driving home. I kept glancing in the rearview mirror. No one was following me. Why was I feeling so paranoid?

But I knew why. The box. I thought of how that man had stared at it when I walked out of the bank. I thought of how the white SUV had followed me. *It was not following you*, I told myself sternly. I thought about the break-in at my apartment. In my mind I saw again my ransacked living room, the torn poster of planets against a starry backdrop. A chill ran down my spine. Why hadn't I hidden the box before I left? Why had I left it sitting in plain sight on the table, practically inviting someone to steal it? My grandfather had kept it locked away for years, and with it in my possession half a day I had carelessly left it exposed on my kitchen table. How could I have been so thoughtless?

My heart was racing as I pulled up to the curb outside my apartment house. I scooped up my violin case and backpack, barely taking time to lock the car behind me. I would never forgive myself if the box was gone.

My fingers shook as I fitted the key into my door. They had never felt so clumsy before. When the door finally swung open, I felt a wave of relief to see the box sitting in the center of the table just where I had left it, catching the light from the window. *Thank god.* I sank onto a chair weak-kneed. In the future I would have to be more careful.

Almost at once my phone rang. I glanced at the number before answering and saw that it was Matt.

"Hey," he said. "I hope you haven't forgotten me. I'm the funny-looking guy who came to your concert last night."

"No, I haven't forgotten you," I said, feeling shy because of what had happed after the concert.

"I texted you."

He had? "Oh, sorry. I've been busy. I forgot to check my phone."

"Are we still on for that movie?"

"Movie?" My brain raced. Had we agreed to go to a movie? I remembered he had suggested it, but I thought it was just a possibility. Something to think about.

"Yeah, Friday night. You didn't forget? Because that would be an awful blow to my ego."

I hesitated. I should probably not encourage him. The relationship had no future. One of us would just get hurt. Last night should never have happened. I had been feeling vulnerable after the death of my grandfather. I hadn't been thinking clearly.

"I'm not sure—"

"It's just a movie. I promise I won't talk during it. I won't laugh at any inappropriate moments. I'll even buy popcorn."

I laughed. He made my qualms seem silly.

"Unless, of course, you don't like popcorn."

Still I hesitated. But I had no excuse not to go, and I didn't want to just say no. Besides, maybe a movie would be fun. Maybe it was just what I needed to take my mind off the box, my grandfather, and Mr. Malinsky.

Matt took my silence for encouragement. "What kind of movie do you like? Romance? Comedy? Horror? Action? Or do you want to be surprised?"

"Are you always this persistent?"

"Yes. Especially when it comes to girls who can pick out Orion's Belt in the sky."

Really, how could I say no to him? "All right. Surprise me."

"Yes!"

CHAPTER 6

When I got off the phone, the box no longer seemed so alarming. It sat there in the center of my table so innocently. Maybe I should just open it and be done with it. I was making too much of it. I reached for the box and gently shook it. It didn't rattle. It was so light it might have been empty. Or it could contain papers. Maybe even photographs. Or a diary. But what if it contained something I would regret finding? Or *unleashing*. I thought of Pandora's box, then pushed that thought away. All the same, I should be careful about opening a box I had been told could be dangerous. If only there were someone who could tell me what was in it.

Later that night before I went to bed it occurred to me that there *was* one person who might know something about the box, my great-aunt Nora, my grandfather's sister who lived in Florida. I had met her when I was ten and she visited us. Now she lived in a retirement community in St. Petersburg. She had not been able to fly to New York for the funeral because it was too far and she had recently broken her hip.

I punched in her number and listened to her phone ring. A second before she picked up, I remembered the time and winced. I probably should not be calling so late.

"This is a surprise," Aunt Nora said. "I was just lying here in bed reading a book. I hope nothing's wrong."

"How are you doing?" I asked.

"Me? Not dancing any jigs, but I can still play a mean game of bridge. How about you, my dear? How are you holding up?"

"I'm okay."

"I do hope you have friends there you can turn to. I know what a loss this is for you. Albert was your rock."

I felt a lump rise in my throat. "The hardest part is sorting through his things."

"You should find someone to help you."

"I can do it myself. That's not really a problem. But there was a break-in . . ."

"A break-in? What do you mean?"

Darn! I shouldn't have told her that. I didn't want to upset her. But now that it had slipped out, I had no choice but to explain. "Someone broke into his apartment. Last Saturday. The day before his funeral." I wouldn't mention my own break-in. No reason to worry her.

"That's terrible. Was anything stolen?"

"I'm not sure."

"Look, if there's anything I can do . . ."

This was my chance to ask. "Actually the reason I called is I thought you might know something about a box my grandfather left for me. It's a small aluminum box that he kept in a safe deposit box at the bank. Do you know anything about it?"

"A box? No, I don't remember anything about a box. What's in it?"

"That's just it. I don't know. He left a letter telling me not to open it."

"How odd. Why would he tell you that?"

"He said it might be dangerous. Anyway, now I'm trying to make up my mind whether to open it or not."

"I'm sorry I can't help you with that. How about money? Do you have enough?"

I didn't want to take Aunt Nora's money. "My tuition's already paid for this term. And I have a scholarship. My grandfather had some investments. I think I'll be fine. But it's kind of you to offer."

"Good. I'm glad to hear he didn't leave you destitute. Albert was never very interested in money."

"You met my mother, didn't you?" I asked.

"I did. It's such a shame you didn't have a chance to know her. She was a really sweet person. Very shy. But she loved your father. I only met her once. They came to visit me soon after they got married. You never saw two people so much in love. Your father was devastated when she died."

"The box belonged to my mother."

"Well, maybe that's why I never heard about it."

"So do you think I should open it?"

"It's the only way you'll know what's in it."

"But my grandfather said it was dangerous."

"Did he explain why?"

"My mother said it was dangerous. Or maybe my father said that. I'm not sure. There was a letter with it."

"I don't know what to tell you, sweetie. If it's dangerous, I suppose you shouldn't open it. Better to be safe than sorry, right?"

"I thought it might have information about my mother in it since it belonged to her."

"Maybe it does."

"I don't know much about her except that she came from California."

"No, I think it was Canada."

"Canada?" This surprised me.

"Yes, I think that's what they told me."

"And they met somewhere in Arizona."

"Yes, that New Age place. Where they sell crystals and whatnot. I can't think of the name right now. You know, where the red rocks are."

"Sedona? I thought that's where they went on their honeymoon." I wondered if Aunt Nora was confused.

"Yes, that's it. Sedona. That's where they met, where they married, and where they spent their honeymoon."

That was strange. My grandfather had told me that they met at a conference in Seattle. And they had married in a small private ceremony here in a chapel at the university. Then they flew to Sedona for their honeymoon. But I didn't want to contradict my great-aunt.

"It all happened so fast," she said. "You hear of people who marry on impulse like that, but how many times does it actually work out?"

"On impulse?" No one had ever mentioned it was on impulse.

"He only knew her ten days. Who can know in ten days if they want to spend the rest of their life with someone?"

"Wait a minute. He only knew her ten days?" Surely that could not be right.

"Didn't your grandfather ever tell you this?"

"No, he—I thought . . ." I thought they had known each other longer. Had my father really jumped into marriage only ten days after meeting my mother? Why had my grandfather never told me this?

"You hear of people going to Vegas and jumping into marriage with someone they just met . . . At least you see it in the movies."

"Why was he in Sedona?" I interrupted.

"I think it had something to do with an eclipse. Or a partial eclipse. Something like that."

That sounded like my father all right.

"But I thought . . ." *I thought he had met her at a conference.* I was sure that was what my grandfather had said. A conference in Seattle.

"I remember how surprised I was when they sent me a postcard with the news. I still have it. And anyway it all worked out. That's all that matters."

"But ten days . . ."

"I had the impression it had something to do with her immigration status or her visa, but I could be wrong about that."

Immigration status? Visa? Surely she could not be correct. And if she was wrong about that, maybe she was wrong about everything else. "I should let you get some sleep," I suggested. "I didn't mean to call so late."

"Well, you call again if you have any more questions or if you just need someone to talk to. I'm so sorry about Albert. It doesn't seem possible he's gone. I always thought he'd outlive me."

After the call ended, I sat there and stared at the box. It glittered like mica under the overhead light. Now even more than before, I was curious about what was inside. It seemed that a great deal I thought I knew about my parents' marriage might not be true after all. Either that or Aunt Nora was growing forgetful in old age. But she had not sounded forgetful—more like someone remembering an alternate reality. The question was, which one was true?

CHAPTER 7

Matt showed up on Friday evening wearing a dark green sweater that brought out his brown eyes. I couldn't help noticing that dimple again when he smiled, and when he leaned forward to give me a quick kiss on the cheek, I caught a whiff of cologne.

"So what movie are we going to see?" I asked.

"You said surprise you, right?"

I rolled my eyes. I hoped there was no ax murderer in it.

When we got to the multiplex, Matt bought the tickets while I glanced over the movie posters, wondering which movie he was taking me to. There was a children's animated feature with talking dogs, a horror movie represented by a knife dripping blood (I hoped it wasn't that one), a crime caper, a romantic comedy, and a science fiction movie with two ominous looking spaceships and the faces of two well-known movie stars.

"I hope you like sci-fi," he said when he joined me. "Did I mention I'm a big fan of *Star Trek* and *Star Wars*? And don't even get me started on *Guardians of the Galaxy*."

"I thought you might choose a crime movie—one with car chases and lots of shooting," I told him.

"Naw—I figure I'll get enough of that at work."

The movie turned out to be about aliens visiting earth in large pod-shaped spaceships and humans' efforts to communicate with them. He had made a good choice. It was a complex story with twists and turns you couldn't see coming. And true to his word, we had popcorn to munch on.

Afterward we went to an ice cream shop and rehashed the movie over ice cream cones. Matt liked the odd octopus-like aliens in the movie, and I liked the efforts of the young woman linguist to communicate with them.

"Don't you wonder what aliens might really look like?" he said. "In so many movies they look like us."

I licked my cone, which was starting to melt. "Doubtful that they would look like us. Odds are against it. What are the chances that life would evolve exactly the same on planets light years apart?"

"And how would they get here, right? They'd have to be far more advanced than us. The movie got that right."

"And then humans would fear them," I said. "Just like in the movie. We're always afraid of what we don't know or understand or can't control."

"Especially our governments and the military. To them everything is a threat."

"My grandfather used to say that any alien civilizations checking us out would be wise to do it at a distance or without drawing attention to themselves."

He smiled ruefully. "Let's just hope they aren't as distrustful and trigger-happy as we are."

* * *

After the ice cream cones, we drove to a park bordering the lake and walked along a path that followed the shoreline. The air was chillier now, and in spite of my lightweight jacket I shivered. Overhead, clouds scudded across the moon. Occasionally a jogger or someone walking a dog on a leash passed us. As we walked, we held hands. Matt's hand felt strong and warm holding mine. The voice in my head that whispered *this won't last* was drowned out by the beating of my heart.

"So what happens after you graduate?" he asked as we paused by a large rock and watched the water lapping at the shore.

There it was—the question I had been dreading. It was only fair to tell him. "Actually I've been accepted to Juilliard. I'm transferring in the spring."

"Wow. New York. Then what happens?"

"I may get a job with an orchestra. Or I might travel and give concerts. Or teach. I haven't decided."

"Would you come back here?" His smile twitched.

"I don't know," I answered truthfully. It was a highly competitive world, and I couldn't be sure I would be good enough. Maybe I would fall on my face. But I had to find out. I owed it to myself, and I owed it to my grandfather.

He sighed.

"It's not like I leave tomorrow."

"Yeah, but . . ." He squinted up at the night sky. "Where was that star again?"

"Over there"—I pointed—"but you can't see it tonight because of the clouds."

"I wish we'd met sooner."

I didn't know what to say. Would it have made any difference if we had met sooner?

"I've never met anyone like you before."

"I'm not so special."

"Of course, you are."

"I bet you say that to all your girlfriends."

His hand flew to his heart. "I'm wounded."

I laughed.

"Do you give all your boyfriends such a rough time?"

"What boyfriends?"

"Really? You're kidding, right?"

"Practicing the violin doesn't leave much time for other things. If you want to be good at it, you have to make sacrifices."

"You've never had a boyfriend? No. I don't believe that."

"Maybe one or two," I conceded.

"But none as hot as me."

I laughed again. He had such a knack for making me laugh.

"I love it when you laugh." He pulled me close and kissed me.

"Matt—" I wanted to warn him that it wouldn't last. I would have to leave for Juilliard in the spring. He understood that, didn't he?

"Look, a shooting star!" he said.

My eyes flew to the sky, dense with slow-moving clouds. There was no shooting star. There were no stars at all. "You're making that up."

"Cross my heart, swear to die."

* * *

It was those kisses. When we started kissing, I forgot about everything else—my qualms, my reservations, my resolutions. They all slipped away. Was this just a reaction to losing my grandfather? I had only known Matt since Sunday. People couldn't fall in love that fast, could they? It wasn't love I told myself. It was more like falling off a cliff or getting hit by a fast moving train. Blindsided. Was that what it had been like for my parents? Had they plunged into marriage barely knowing each other? Was Aunt Nora right?

We were back at my apartment standing in the dark by the door kissing. We had gotten no farther into the apartment. I pulled back and tried to catch my breath. It was all happening so fast. We barely knew each other. What were we doing?

"Do you think a person can know after only ten days that the person they are with is who they want to be with for life?" I asked in a breathless rush.

"What?" He sounded as dazed as I felt.

I repeated the question.

"I think it's been more like five," he said, "but who's counting?"

"Be serious. I'm talking about my mom and dad, not us."

"Oh, well then. That's different."

"My great-aunt said they only knew each other ten days before they married."

"Maybe that's all it took. Maybe your dad thought to himself, why waste time getting to know each other? We can get to know each other after we're married."

He was teasing now. I tried to explain. If I could keep talking, maybe my head would stop spinning and I could think clearly.

"I knew they didn't know each other long before they married, but my grandfather never told me it was just ten days. I guess I always assumed it was longer."

"Ten days, huh? So we have five to go?"

"That's not what I—"

"What's that?" He nodded at the box sitting on the table, silver in the pale light from the window. It almost looked like the light came from within, as if the box were softly glowing. It was beautiful sitting there like that in the dark.

"Remember that key?"

"*That's* what was in the safe deposit box?" He was all attention now, walking toward the box. "So what's in it?"

I followed him. "I don't know. I haven't opened it."

"Why not? Don't you want to know what's in it?"

"My grandfather thought I shouldn't open it." I reached up and turned on the hanging lamp over the table. Then I smoothed out the letter for him to read.

"What do you suppose is in it?" he asked after reading the letter.

"I have no idea."

He reached for the box and shook it gently, just as I had done. "It sounds empty."

"Yeah, I thought so too. But why would my mother say it was dangerous if it's empty?"

"Is that some kind of writing on it?" He held the box up to the light and examined the markings.

"I don't think so. I think it's just some sort of design."

"Why would your mom have left you something she considered dangerous?"

"Technically she didn't. It's my grandfather who left it for me."

"Your grandfather then."

I didn't want to blame my grandfather. He had been trying to do the right thing. "Maybe it's not dangerous. Maybe it has photos in it. Or letters."

"Then why can't we hear them?"

"I don't know. Maybe there's filler in it—like bubble wrap."

"If it *is* something dangerous, maybe you should keep it in a bank vault, like your grandfather suggested."

"I thought if I put it here where I could see it, maybe I could figure out what to do with it."

"Want me to open it?" He arched an eyebrow and grinned.

"No," I said quickly.

"It looks like ordinary sealing tape. It shouldn't be too hard to remove."

"But I haven't decided I want to open it. I wish there were someone I could ask about it. I called my great-aunt, but she didn't know anything about it."

"Well, if it *is* dangerous, this may not be the safest place to keep it. You had a break-in just recently, in case you've forgotten. What if it gets stolen? Then you might never know what was in it."

"Yeah, I thought about that. In fact, I thought someone was following me . . ."

"When?"

"When I was driving home from the bank yesterday with the box. There was this white SUV. And later when I was ready to come home after violin practice, I had this feeling I was being followed."

"Were you?"

"I didn't see anyone."

He frowned and ran a hand through his curly hair. "Why didn't you say something before?"

"Well, it was probably just my imagination."

He began to pace. "Suppose someone knows about this box. In fact, maybe that's why they broke into your apartment. Did you think of that?"

"Matt—" I didn't want him to get carried away. I doubted there was any connection between the box and someone breaking into my apartment. Who could have known about it? At the time *I* didn't even know about it.

"And the break-in at your grandfather's apartment—" he continued, still pacing. "Maybe this is what they were looking for."

I shook my head. "No, it's just a coincidence."

"How can you be sure? Have you asked yourself why your grandfather gave his friend Joseph Malinsky the key instead of giving it to you or leaving it somewhere for you to find?"

I didn't want to believe the break-ins had anything to do with the box. That might mean Mr. Malinsky's death was somehow connected to it and therefore connected to *me*. The thought was unsettling. Could Matt be right? Was it possible something valuable was in the box and someone knew that? Someone willing to kill for it?

"It was probably just my imagination that someone was following me," I repeated, but I was less certain now.

By the time Matt left, I had promised to let him know if I thought someone was following me or call 911. When I was alone again, I made myself a cup of tea and studied the box. I ran my fingers across those odd markings just below the tape.

They weren't really a design. There was no pattern to them. They were tiny random lines and swirls. Almost like a language I didn't know.

I spent the next hour searching online to see if I could find another box like it. Finally around one I gave up and went to bed. As I lay there trying to fall asleep, it occurred to me that I could post a photo of the box online and see if anyone recognized it. But if someone *had* killed Mr. Malinsky to get to the box, posting a picture of it would be risky. No, until I knew more about the box, I should be careful about drawing attention to it.

CHAPTER 8

The next morning as I sipped my coffee and contemplated the box, I wondered if maybe an antique dealer would be able to tell me if the box was valuable. It wasn't an antique, but antique dealers knew about unusual objects. At least it was worth a try, and since it was Saturday I had the time. With a few more keystrokes I found a listing online for an antique dealer in Syracuse.

After a quick phone call to make sure the shop was open, I was on my way. As I drove, I kept glancing in my rearview mirror to be sure I wasn't being followed. It was silly, I told myself. No one knew about the box. The break-ins and Mr. Malinsky's death most likely had nothing to do with the box. And the white van that I had thought was following me that day had probably not been following me after all.

My destination turned out to be a small shop tucked between a massage parlor and an adult bookstore in a seedy section of the city. A small bell over the door jangled when I walked in. Inside I found myself surrounded by a clutter of dusty objects lining shelves in narrow aisles—vases, lamps, figurines, old books, dolls, dishes, and even a birdcage. I was the only customer in the shop. In response to the bell a shifty-eyed man with a ponytail sidled out of a door in the back. He looked annoyed at being disturbed. Maybe he had been napping in the back or smoking a joint. I thought I caught a whiff of marijuana.

He looked me over suspiciously. It was no wonder he had no customers. If it hadn't been for the box, I would have turned and walked out.

"Mr. Sadler?" I said.

"Yeah?"

"We talked earlier on the phone. I called you about a box."

He heaved an impatient sigh. "You got it with you?"

I slipped off the backpack, careful not to bump against any of the antiques. All I needed was to knock down a Chinese vase or a mermaid lamp. I was pretty sure this was a you-break-it, you-buy-it kind of shop.

I lifted the box from my backpack and set it on the counter, where he regarded it with a bored expression.

I tried not to let that discourage me. "Have you seen anything like it before?"

He shrugged. "What's inside?"

"I don't know."

"Where'd you get it?"

"From my grandfather. He died recently."

"Well, I can't tell you much about it if I can't see inside."

"You can't tell just from looking at it if it's valuable?"

He frowned and ran his long fingers across the sealing

tape. Then he put on a pair of wire-rimmed glasses and looked at it closer. He tapped the markings. "Odd design."

"Can you tell me what it's made of?" I asked. "At first I thought it was aluminum, but—"

"It's not aluminum." He rapped on it lightly with his knuckles.

I resisted the urge to snatch it back. "Then what?"

He scratched his head. "Something synthetic." Clearly the box didn't impress him.

Disappointed, I reached for it, but quick as lightning he planted his hands on both sides of it, stopping me. "What I could do is snap a photo of it and post it."

I shook my head. "No thank you."

He shrugged and held up his hands in surrender. "Suit yourself."

I put the box back in my backpack. It had been a wasted trip.

"Is that your car?" he asked, frowning toward the door. "Because if it is, that's a no parking zone."

I glanced back at the door of the shop and saw through the glass a white SUV parked at the curb. My heart jumped into my mouth. It had not been there when I entered the shop. I would have noticed it.

"No, it's not my car." I tried to stay calm. My mind raced as I zipped my backpack closed. I would have to walk past the SUV unless there was a back way out. Would the shop owner think it strange if I asked? Or maybe I should just stay a little longer, browse around the shop, and see if the SUV left. But what if it didn't leave or whoever was in it decided to come into the shop? No, better to go, I decided. And better not to ask about a back door. It would make the owner suspicious. He didn't look like the sort to help a woman in distress.

My heart was pounding as I threaded my way through the shop's narrow aisles to the door with my backpack. Maybe it wasn't the same SUV, I told myself. There must be lots of white SUVs in the city. So was it just parked there or was someone sitting in it? Because of the tinted windshield, I couldn't see if anyone was inside.

Taking a deep breath, I pushed open the shop door. I half expected someone to jump out of the SUV and challenge me, but no one did. My heart thumping in my chest, I walked as rapidly as I could to where my car was parked in a small municipal lot a block down the street. Once I was inside, my hand trembled as I turned the key in the ignition. Would the white SUV follow me? If it did, should I phone Matt and tell him someone was following me? But that would mean bothering him while he was on duty. And if I called 911, what would I tell the operator? Maybe this SUV wasn't the one that had followed me before, and if it wasn't, I would look like a fool. Was I going to get alarmed every time I saw a white SUV?

As I drove away, I watched in my rearview mirror to see if the SUV appeared. It didn't. Then a chilling thought struck me. If it was the same SUV, how had whoever was inside known where I would be? Had they followed me earlier that morning? I didn't think they had. Did they have some way of tracking me? A shiver ran down my spine.

Thoroughly spooked, I took wrong turns and a roundabout route home just in case I was being followed. But there was no sign of the white SUV. After I calmed down, I decided not to tell Matt about it. He would want to know why I hadn't phoned him. But I couldn't be sure it was the same SUV. I was letting my imagination carry me away. I really needed to stop being so paranoid.

CHAPTER 9

So far Matt had not told me anything more about Mr. Malinsky's death. All I knew was that it had been a home invasion and the intruders had cut his throat. His funeral would be held Sunday, and I had been debating whether to go. On the one hand, it seemed too soon after my father's funeral to attend another funeral, but on the other I felt I should go. It seemed like the right thing to do. And if I went, I might be able to find out something more about the circumstances of his death.

When I entered the funeral home, I felt nervous and almost turned around and left. Everyone stood about in small groups, and at first glance I saw no one I knew. I peeked into the next room and felt relieved when I saw the casket was closed. Of course, it would be. A slashed throat is not the sort of thing you want mourners to see. I noticed two women, one older, one younger, greeting people, so I waited in line to offer my condolences. The older woman turned out to be a niece of Mr. Malinsky's and the younger her daughter. They had come from out of town for the funeral. The niece smiled politely when I told her my grandfather had played checkers with Mr. Malinsky and had been a colleague of his at the university. The daughter looked bored and kept glancing at her cell phone.

"I couldn't believe it when I heard about his . . . death." I hesitated to say *murder*. It seemed somehow heartless to say the word to a relative.

"His health wasn't good," the niece said. "Still, no one expected him to die like this."

"Do the police know who did it?" I asked, taking advantage of the opportunity to troll for information.

"They think it was drug addicts. Part of this opioid crisis. I just hope they catch whoever it was."

Her duty done, she turned to the couple behind me, my cue to move on. Maybe it was a mistake to have come. The sight of the casket surrounded by flowers depressed me. It reminded me of my grandfather's funeral the previous weekend, and it didn't look like I was going to learn anything new.

As I stood there trying to decide whether to duck out or stay, I noticed a plump middle-aged woman in a dark blue pantsuit slide into a pew in the back of the room. Apparently I wasn't the only person in the room who didn't have a group to join. That decided me. I walked over and sat down beside her, hoping to look less conspicuous than I did standing alone.

"Are you a relative?" I asked.

"Me? Goodness no, I'm just a neighbor. I live next door to the Professor. *Lived* I should say since he's not alive anymore. I've always kept an eye out for the old gent. When my husband passed away—God rest his soul—the Professor was very kind to me. How about you, dear?"

"He was a friend of my grandfather's."

"It's a crime what happened to him. It's getting so no one is safe anymore. I hope they catch whoever did this."

"I heard they were drug addicts."

She looked around warily, then leaning closer, whispered, "I saw who did it. It wasn't drug addicts."

"Really?" Could I have stumbled upon some important information after all?

She nodded. "Or one of them anyway. There may have been more than one."

"Did you tell the police?"

"They weren't interested."

Not interested? How could that be? Surely if she had seen someone, they would want to know.

"What did this man look like?" I asked.

"Dressed in black, like those men in the TV movie. You know the one I mean. And he didn't look like a drug addict either." She nodded knowingly.

"How do you know he was the killer?"

"I saw him coming out of the Professor's apartment, and no one saw the Professor alive again after that."

I saw why the police might have been skeptical. Someone else could have gone into the apartment after the man she had seen. There was no way to be sure he was the last person to see Mr. Malinsky alive.

"Who found him?" I asked.

"The building super. But that was the next morning after he didn't show up to teach his classes. Someone got concerned, I suppose."

"Did the man see you?"

"Well, yes. But he looked away right away. I thought it a little strange at the time because I never saw him before, but it didn't occur to me he might have just murdered the Professor. How was I to know?"

"You couldn't," I agreed.

We had to stop talking then because the minister had just stepped up to the podium to give the eulogy. I wondered if the woman beside me had indeed seen the killer or just someone who had been visiting Mr. Malinsky. She had seemed certain the man wasn't a drug addict, but if a drug addict hadn't killed him, then who had? And was there any connection to the break-in at my apartment and the one at my grandfather's? Were these events all somehow related, as Matt had suggested? And were they linked by the box that had belonged to my mother?

After the service Barb Peterson—the woman claiming she had seen the killer—asked me if I could give her a lift to the cemetery. She said her car was low on gas but she would like to attend. I had planned to leave once the service was over, but giving her a ride to the cemetery might give me the opportunity to learn more from her, so I agreed.

"Do you think you might recognize the man if you saw him again?" I asked as we crawled along in the small procession of cars making their way to the cemetery.

"I'm not sure. I only saw him for a split second before he turned his face away. I should have known right then he was up to no good."

"But you think there was more than one man?"

"Well, there might have been one waiting in his car—the getaway driver."

"Did you see his car?" I immediately thought of the white SUV.

"No, my windows don't look down on the parking area."

"Oh." I tried to hide my disappointment.

"But there still could have been a getaway driver," she insisted. "It stands to reason."

I saw why the police had been skeptical about her story—a man in black with a hypothetical getaway driver in a vehicle she hadn't seen. There were too many assumptions there. Still, maybe she *had* seen the killer.

During the gravesite ceremony I stood beside Barb, who kept dabbing her eyes with a tissue, and wished that I hadn't come. I looked around at the mourners and wondered if the murderer was there. In movies and TV crime shows murderers often show up at their victims' funerals. But no one looked like a murderer. We sat on folding chairs under a canopy and bowed our heads as the minister said a prayer. I was glad for the canopy since it looked like it might soon rain.

Barb wanted to talk to Mr. Malinsky's niece and her daughter before we left, so I walked back up the embankment to my car to wait for her. I wondered if she would tell them about the man she had seen leaving Mr. Malinsky's apartment. I assumed he hadn't been at the funeral or she would have said something.

Just as I reached my car, a young man about my age caught up with me. He was tall with reddish brown hair and pale skin with freckles. He was a little out of breath from the climb up the embankment.

"Were you one of his students?" he asked.

I shook my head. "No, he was a friend of my grandfather's."

"You look familiar. Do I know you?"

"Do you go to the university?"

"Yeah. Majoring in astronomy. Malinsky was my mentor."

"I'm in the music department."

He snapped his fingers. "I bet I've seen you on campus."

"Maybe. So you knew Professor Malinsky well?"

"He's the reason I'm majoring in astronomy. When I was a freshman, I didn't have a clue what I wanted to do. Then I took his course. He opened my eyes. If it hadn't been for him, I'd probably have ended up an English major." He grinned and shook his head as if to suggest he had narrowly avoided making a huge mistake.

"He was your mentor?"

"Yeah. I can't believe he's gone." He held out his hand. "Kevin Burke."

I shook it. "Lauren Ferguson."

"You here alone?" he asked, glancing back at the stragglers near the gravesite. I spotted Barb in her dark blue pantsuit breaking away from the cluster still milling about the grave.

"I'm waiting for someone."

He squinted again at the stragglers. "Want to catch a cup of coffee sometime? Now if you're free."

I was caught off-guard. It seemed odd to ask someone he just met out for coffee. Who picked up women at a funeral? I shook my head. "I'm seeing someone."

He nodded, not meeting my eyes. Barb was trudging up the embankment toward us now, saving us from an awkward situation.

"Well, that must be your ride," he said. "See you around." With a backward wave of his arm, he abruptly took off toward a nearby car. Maybe he had been embarrassed by my brush off, but what did he expect?

"Who was that?" Barb asked as she reached me, a hand pressed to her chest, out of breath after climbing the incline.

"One of Mr. Malinsky's students."

"I hope I didn't scare him off."

I smiled. "Your timing was perfect."

CHAPTER 10

That evening I met Matt at the mall, and we claimed a table in the food court near Starbucks. Over lattes I told him about the funeral and Barb.

"She said she *saw* who did it," I explained. "But the police weren't interested."

"Then there must have been some reason," Matt said, "like she wasn't a credible witness."

"I don't think she got a good look at his face," I admitted. "She said he turned away."

"There you go."

"Anyway she didn't think he was a drug addict."

"And why not?" He had a half smile on his face, eyebrow raised.

"He didn't look like a drug addict."

"And what does a drug addict look like?"

I ignored that. "She said he was dressed in black."

Matt rolled his eyes. "Does she watch TV much?"

He was right, of course. It didn't sound very convincing. What were the odds that she had really seen the killer? Maybe she was just a lonely middle-aged woman who wanted a little attention. I sipped my latte. I hadn't mentioned Kevin Burke. I didn't want Matt to think I had encouraged him. Besides, what was there to say? A nerdy-looking astronomy major had asked me out, and I had turned him down.

"Why'd you go anyway?" he asked.

"He was my grandfather's friend." I could have added that I had been looking for answers. It wasn't like *he* was giving me any.

"Look, there's something odd about this murder," he said, turning serious. "I'm not so sure it was opioid-related."

"What was odd?"

He sighed. "They found some fentanyl in his medicine cabinet."

"So?"

"So an opioid addict wouldn't have left it there."

That meant maybe Barb had been right after all about the killer not being a drug addict. "If it wasn't opioid-related, what was it?"

"Might have been just a burglary gone bad. Maybe they were after money." He sounded glum and wasn't making eye contact. What was he not telling me?

He sighed again. "Look, I'm not sure, but the feds might be involved."

In my mind I saw Barb's man in black. Was it possible that she really had seen the killer? Before I could ask any questions, we were interrupted by one of Matt's friends as he pulled up a chair to join us. He was tall and skinny with frizzy black hair and a wide smile.

"Hey, what's happening?" he said.

Matt groaned. "This is TJ," he said. "TJ—Lauren."

"New girlfriend?" TJ stuck his hand out and I shook it.

"Don't you have someplace else to be?" Matt asked.

"Nope. Just got off work."

"He works at the Apple store. A geek."

"So, Malone, you finally found a girl who would go out with you?"

"Don't start. If you mess this up for me, I swear . . ."

"Did he tell you about his last girlfriend?" TJ said, turning to me. "What was her name? Matt, help me out here. Cheryl? Shirley?"

"Don't you have something to do?"

TJ snapped his fingers. "Sherry. That was it. She dumped him. Did he tell you about that?"

"She didn't dump me. It was a mutual thing. We decided to break up."

TJ rolled his eyes. "You keep telling yourself that."

"Did you come here to torment me or to hit on the new barista?"

TJ sighed. "Hey, don't knock it. She smiled at me yesterday. I think I'm making progress. So how did you two meet?"

Matt and I exchanged glances.

"My apartment was broken into," I offered.

TJ threw Matt a long look. "*Really?*"

Matt looked embarrassed.

"So what do you do, Lauren?" TJ asked, enjoying Matt's discomfort.

"She's a student at the university," Matt said. "Now why don't you go buy a coffee and see if you can make any headway with that barista."

TJ stayed where he was. He looked at me expectantly, waiting for my answer.

"I'm studying the violin," I said.

He looked at Matt. "She did say violin, didn't she? Did I hear that right?"

Matt drummed his fingers on the table and looked at the ceiling.

TJ grinned broadly. "This should be interesting."

Matt shot him a look.

"Coffee—right," TJ said, rising. "Anyone want anything?"

I glanced toward the line of people waiting at the counter as he walked away and spotted the barista—slim as a model, big dark sultry eyes, and an attitude.

Matt sighed. "Sorry about that. He thinks we're still in high school."

"Why would the feds be involved?" I asked.

"I said *maybe*. Because suddenly everyone has gone mum. No one will tell me anything."

"But why would the feds be involved?"

"I don't know. That's what's so strange."

"Maybe these break-ins aren't connected."

"But what if they *are*?"

"Why would they want a box my mother left for me that's been locked away in a vault for twenty years? How would they even know about it?"

Before he could answer, TJ came swaggering back, a big grin on his face. "Man, she almost smiled at me."

He had barely sat down when the barista stormed up behind him, an Amazon in platform heels, eyes blazing. She slapped a twenty-dollar bill on the table. "What's this?"

"A tip?" TJ suggested.

"For a two-dollar cup of coffee? Are you trying to *buy* me?"

"I wouldn't do that." He sounded wounded.

"Because if you are, I'm way out of your league."

"You can't blame a guy for trying."

She glared at Matt and me. "Are these your friends?"

"Yeah. This is Matt, and this is Matt's new girlfriend."

"Lauren," I said.

TJ saw his opportunity and leaned forward. "And you are—?"

"Joy." She tossed it at him like a grenade.

A wide grin broke across his face.

"You think that's funny?"

His smile vanished in an instant. "No, ma'am."

"We can't help what our parents name us," she said.

"That's the truth," TJ agreed. "They come up with some godawful names."

"You think I have a godawful name?"

"Course not."

"So what's *your* name?" she demanded.

"Me? TJ."

"What's it stand for?"

He looked uncomfortable. "Nothing. It's just TJ. That's my name. Matt, tell her."

She pivoted, ready to stalk away.

"Wait a minute," TJ said. "It stands for Thomas Jefferson."

"Is that the truth?"

"Absolutely. Look at this face. Would I lie? Especially to a beautiful woman like you?"

She rolled her eyes and strode back to the bar. He watched her go.

"I think she likes me."

"You gave her a twenty-dollar tip?" Matt said.

"It worked, didn't it?" TJ pocketed the twenty.

At that moment I noticed a tall young man with red hair opening up a laptop at a table on the edge of the food court. It was Kevin Burke, the guy I'd met at the cemetery that afternoon who tried to ask me out for coffee. He looked up, saw me, and flung up his hand awkwardly in greeting, then hunkered down at his laptop.

"Someone you know?" Matt asked.

"Not really. He was at the funeral for Mr. Malinsky today."

Matt studied him. "A university student?"

"Yes, one of Malinsky's students."

"You talked to him?"

"Just for a few moments."

"Did he ask you out?" TJ asked.

Matt shot him a warning look.

I hesitated, unsure how to answer. It was just my luck that Kevin Burke would turn up at the food court.

"Ooo, competition," TJ said.

"He was just being friendly," I said.

"Yeah, sure."

"Astronomy major?" Matt asked, eyeing Kevin again.

"Yes." I sipped my latte. "I'm sure he didn't murder Mr. Malinsky, if that's what you're thinking."

TJ almost choked on his coffee. "Murder?"

"You'd vouch for him?" Matt said. "Someone you don't know?"

"Well, he looks harmless."

We all looked at him. He sat there oblivious to the fact that we were staring at him. And talking about him. At least he was far enough away to be out of earshot.

"It's the harmless-looking ones you have to watch out for," TJ said. "You never watched *Law and Order*?"

"You can't picture him committing murder?" Matt asked.

"No," I said. "I can't."

"Or trashing your apartment?"

"No."

"Or your grandfather's?"

"Okay, what's this all about?" TJ said. He looked at me. "Someone trashed your apartment?"

"That's how we met." I glanced at Matt.

"How's that connect to murder?" TJ asked. "What am I missing here?"

"It doesn't," I said. "It doesn't connect to murder at all."

"You know, if you'd been at home that day, it might have turned out different," Matt said, watching me sip my latte.

The image of Mr. Malinsky with his throat slit rose unbidden in my mind. I quickly pushed it away. Was Matt right? Would I have gotten my throat slashed if I'd been at home?

"Did you put that box in a safe place?"

"Yes." I reached under the table and touched my backpack, reassuring myself that it was still there, leaning against my leg. If anyone broke into my apartment, they wouldn't find it.

"What box?" TJ said, looking from me to Max.

"Something her mother left her."

TJ rolled his eyes. "This just keeps getting weirder."

"Matt thinks that's why someone broke into my apartment," I explained. "He thinks someone was looking for the box."

"Well, while you two Sherlocks figure this out, I'm going to try my luck again," he said, pushing back his chair and standing.

As he walked away, Matt placed his hand over mine and gave me that lopsided smile that made my heart beat faster. "Did he really ask you for a date?"

"More like coffee." My eye dropped to my Starbucks cup. I was glad that I was sitting there with Matt and not with Kevin Burke.

"He probably knows a lot more than me about stars," Matt said with another glance at Kevin.

"And he probably hates Beethoven."

Matt squeezed my hand. "Long-haired dude in a rock band, right? Plays a mean bass?"

"Yeah, that's the guy."

"Bet I've watched more episodes of *Star Trek* than he has."

"You might be right about that."

TJ was grinning from ear to ear when he came back a few minutes later. He waved a scrap of paper triumphantly. "Got her phone number. I told you she likes me."

I touched my backpack under the table again. It was a nice feeling to be in the warm brightly lit court, surrounded by the scraping of chairs on the tile floor and the buzz of voices in conversation. After having attended the funeral earlier in the day, it felt good to be in the midst of life. I felt sorry for Kevin Burke, sitting alone in a corner with his laptop.

We left the mall thirty minutes later. While TJ trotted off to find his car, Matt and I lingered in the shadow of the building. There was a chill in the air, and I shivered in my lightweight jacket.

"You want to come back to my place?" he asked.

I had not yet seen his apartment, which I knew he shared with several roommates, including his brother who worked at Mama Mia's.

"Tempting, but I have classes tomorrow."

"And I have to work." He sighed and pulled me closer. I felt his breath near my ear. If we started kissing, I wasn't sure I could hold out against that invitation to his apartment.

Suddenly he froze.

"What?"

"Shh."

Someone had just emerged from the sliding glass door of the mall. In the light spilling out from the mall I recognized Kevin Burke, his laptop tucked under his arm. He looked around but apparently didn't see us standing there in the shadow of the building. I held my breath. Neither of us moved until he walked away. We watched until he climbed into a car, turned on his headlights, and drove away.

"Do you think he was following us?" I asked.

"Do you?"

"Why would he follow us?"

"Maybe he likes you."

"Or maybe he just happened to finish whatever he was doing on his laptop—a paper or something."

"Right," Matt said. "Nothing stalker about that at all."

I punched him lightly on the chest. "He's not a stalker." But it did bother me. I didn't like the fact that Kevin Burke had turned up at the food court. I didn't like that at all. I looked around the parking lot, uneasy, but it seemed quiet, almost deserted, just a scattering of cars.

CHAPTER 11

I was driving to the campus the next day when a cell phone rang—an odd jingly tune, not at all like any of my own. While keeping my eyes on the road, I tried to locate the source of the sound. Finally I spotted the phone lying on the floor in front of the passenger seat. I knew right away it must belong to Barb Peterson, the woman I had met the day before at the funeral who had ridden with me to the cemetery. She must have dropped it while she was in my car.

At the next traffic light I reached down and retrieved the phone. The next time it started to ring, I pulled over to the curb and answered it. It was Barb, and she was relieved I had found her phone. She had been worried that she had lost it at the cemetery. She gave me her address, and I promised to stop by later and return it.

It was late afternoon after violin practice when I drove to her apartment building, another crumbling old red brick relic much like my grandfather's. I had to buzz her apartment to use the elevator. When I stepped off on the 5th floor, I noticed the yellow crime scene tape across the apartment door next to hers. That would be Mr. Malinsky's apartment. The sight of the tape made me feel uneasy. I wondered if the tenants on the floor were used to seeing it now or if it still unsettled them, as it did me.

Barb came to the door in baggy sweatpants, a loose lime green T-shirt with a picture of a cat's face above the word *purrfect*, and fuzzy pink slippers on her feet.

"Thank you so much!" she said, reaching for the phone I held out to her. "I thought I had lost it." She stood there, holding the door open. "Oh, come in. You've got a minute, haven't you?"

I hadn't intended to go in, but now that I was there it seemed only polite to give her a few minutes of my time. It wasn't as if there was something I had to do.

Once inside, I was surprised by the number of cats she had. At a glance I counted half a dozen. A calico blinked at me from the back of the sofa, a black cat strolled over to circle my legs, meowing, and a fluffy orange cat eyed me narrowly from the windowsill. More lurked in the background.

Barb swept some newspapers off the sofa so I could sit down. As soon as I did, the black cat leaped up beside me.

"That's Lucifer," she said. "He's a pistol, aren't you, Lucy?"

I petted Lucifer and he curled up beside me, eyes half closed, content to have found someone to pet him.

"You're my second visitor today," Barb said, plucking up a small yellow toy from the floor. "I don't know when there's been so much excitement around here."

"Did the police come back?" I asked.

"No, that young man was here—you know, the one who was at the funeral."

"Kevin Burke?" I was surprised. I didn't realize she had met him.

"Yes, such a nice young man. Lucifer liked him too."

"Why was he here?"

"Oh, I think he felt badly about what happened to the Professor and wanted someone to talk to."

"But how did he know about you?"

Lucifer looked up at me and meowed to let me know I should continue to pet him.

"Oh, I found him out in the hall wandering about. Poor thing. He said he just had to see where it happened."

"But how did he get into the building?"

She shrugged. "I suppose someone let him in. It happens all the time."

Well, that explained how the murderer could get in. So much for building security.

"He's a very sweet young man. I think the Professor's death was quite a blow to him."

"Did you tell him about the man in black?"

She nodded vigorously. "I did. He thought the police should have listened to me. He said he thought what I saw was very important. I'm an *eye witness*." She sat a little straighter.

So how was Kevin Burke connected to all this? He had turned up three times now within two days. Was he an astronomy student as he claimed or was he something else?

"Did he tell you anything about himself?" I asked.

She bit her lip, thinking. "We mostly talked about the

Professor. He told me how he went into astronomy because of the Professor."

So he had told Barb the same story he had told me. As I replayed it in my head, it began to sound less convincing, maybe because he paraded it out a little too easily.

I stayed another five minutes, then took my leave, to Barb's disappointment, turning down her offer of a piece of coffee cake.

When I was in the hall again, I found myself staring at the yellow tape stretched across Mr. Malinsky's door. I wondered what the crime scene looked like on the other side of the door. Had the police left things as they found them, or had they cleaned up? Had the apartment been ransacked? Were there blood stains? Where was Mr. Malinsky when he was attacked? Was he at the door? If he was, that would suggest he was attacked when he opened it. Or was he someplace else in the apartment after unwittingly admitting his killer? Had the police found anything? And why was the FBI involved? They only got involved in situations where federal laws had been violated, didn't they? There was so much unexplained about his murder.

No one else was in the hall, so I reached out and turned the knob. Of course, it was locked. What had I expected? The police would not have been so careless as to leave it open. I wondered if Kevin Burke had tried the door too. I glanced about, hoping there were no surveillance cameras. Why didn't I think of that before? I hurried away then, not wanting anyone to see me lingering outside Mr. Malinsky's door. It might look suspicious, and I didn't want to draw attention to myself.

By the time I got to my car, I had my phone out and was googling Kevin Burke. Unfortunately there were at least a dozen people with that name. I saw no quick answers about who he was. Which brought me back to the question of why he was snooping about. Because I didn't believe that story about feeling the need to see where it happened. It rang false. Maybe Kevin Burke wasn't who he said he was.

CHAPTER 12

I decided the best way to track down Kevin Burke might be through the astronomy department, so during my lunch hour the next day I stopped by the Space Sciences Building. Mrs. Calhoun had worked in the office for years and knew me from when my grandfather taught in the department.

I found her sitting at her desk, her greying hair pulled back in a no-nonsense bun and blue eyes looking out through bifocal glasses attached to a cord around her neck. She broke into a smile when she saw me.

"Why, Lauren. This is a surprise. What brings you here?"

"I'm looking for someone," I told her. "Kevin Burke. He's a student in this department. We were supposed to meet and talk, but I lost his phone number. We met at the funeral last weekend."

She looked stricken at mention of the funeral. "Poor Professor Malinsky. We're all still in a state of shock."

"I know. I can't believe he's gone."

"And the way he died!" She shuddered.

I really didn't want to talk about the way he died, so I tried to shift the conversation back to Kevin. "I thought you might have Kevin Burke's phone number. He was one of Professor Malinsky's students."

She frowned. "I don't recollect all the names, but then they come and go so quickly. I gave up a long time ago trying to remember them all."

"He's tall and skinny. Red hair." I hoped describing him would jog her memory.

She shook her head. "Sorry. I wish I could help you."

"That's okay." I had struck out but decided to ask if she knew anything about the police investigation since I was there. "Did the police come and ask you any questions about Professor Malinsky?"

She brightened. "As a matter of fact, they did. Twice in fact. They asked if I knew anyone who might have wanted to hurt him. Can you imagine? Who would want to hurt Professor Malinsky? Everyone liked him."

"He came to my grandfather's funeral."

"Yes, I know. It's so sad. First your grandfather and then Professor Malinsky." She looked around the room. Another secretary was busy on a computer and two student workers by the wall were huddled together with a pile of papers they were marking or sorting. She lowered her voice. "Actually they asked about you too."

"Me?" I stared at her. Why would the police have been asking questions about me?

"The second time. I mean the second guy. He was different from the first."

"Are you sure he was with the police?" I asked uneasily, thinking of the white SUV.

"Of course. What else would he have been?"

I let that pass. "What did he want to know?"

"If I knew you."

"That's all?"

"Well, yes, I think so. I told him of course I knew you. Your father used to teach here. It struck me as odd that he would ask about you, but I assume he asked because your grandfather and Professor Malinsky were friends. I'm sure it's nothing to be concerned about."

She may have been sure, but I wasn't. Why would someone be asking about me? Was it connected to the break-in at my apartment? Was it connected to the box?

My mind was churning when I left the Space Sciences Building a few minutes later. I had forty-five minutes yet before my next class. There was still time to grab some lunch, so I walked to the Campus Corner. The place was packed and loud. I saw right off that it was going to be hard to find a table free, but since my stomach was growling, I stood in line and got a salad and a bowl of soup. Holding my tray, I scanned the room again for a table. That's when I spotted Kevin Burke sitting by himself hunched over his laptop. I could hardly believe my luck. I made a beeline across the room with my tray and slid into the empty chair across from him. I thought he would be pleased, but instead he looked up startled, then glanced around the room in alarm.

"You don't mind if I join you, do you?" I asked.

"What are you doing here?"

"Having lunch."

"I'm kind of busy."

"I wanted to talk to you. I have a few questions to ask you."

He looked apprehensive. "About what?"

"Why did you go see Barb Peterson, for starters."

"What?" He looked ready to jump up and run out of the cafeteria.

"Mr. Malinsky's neighbor—the cat lady. Why did you go see her?"

"I didn't—"

"Oh, that's right. You just happened to turn up in her hallway."

He looked frantically around again. "What are you doing here?"

"I told you. Having lunch." I started eating my salad.

"We shouldn't be seen together."

"Why not?"

"They're watching me."

"Who's watching you?"

"How the hell do I know? FBI, CIA, NSA, Department of Homeland Security, some secret branch of the government no one knows about. You tell me."

"Is your name really Kevin Burke?"

"Of course, that's my name. Why would you ask a question like that?"

"Because I just came from the astronomy department and one of the secretaries there who's a friend of mine said she's never heard of you."

"So what? It's a big department."

"Not really."

He looked nervous now. "They're probably following you too."

I thought of the white SUV, then resolutely pushed it out of my mind. It would only make him more paranoid if I told him about the SUV. "You didn't answer my question. Were you really a student of Malinsky's?"

"All right. You win. I give up." He threw his hands in the air in surrender. "I wasn't actually one of his students, but my roommate was."

I felt a rush of satisfaction. My hunch had been right. He wasn't one of Malinsky's students.

"So what you said at the funeral about Malinsky being your mentor and influencing your choice of major wasn't true?"

"I'm in journalism. Look, how often does a professor get murdered? There's a story here. I know there is. And someone's trying to bury it. If I can get to the bottom of it, I could scoop it on my blog. Don't you see? This could be my big break."

A *journalism* student? His *blog*? Well, that explained a lot. "That's why you went to the funeral? And why you went to see Barb Peterson?"

His eyes darted around the room. "Seriously, I don't think we should be seen together. Someone's following me."

"Well, someone's following me too."

He stared at me. "Who? What does he look like?"

I shrugged. "I don't know. So who do you think murdered Mr. Malinsky? What have you found out?"

"I told you. I don't have a clue. They're trying to bury it."

"Who's trying to bury it?"

"I told you. *They.* I don't know who they are. Do you think they wear ID tags?"

"Maybe it was just drug addicts."

He shook his head. "No, it's more than that. He *knew* something. This is big. Really big."

"So what's your theory? Why would someone murder an aging professor of astronomy? What could he have possibly known that would be a threat to anyone?"

He looked furtively around the room and lowered his voice. "Aliens," he said in a stage whisper.

"Really?" I tried to keep my face expressionless.

"Well, I can't be sure, but it makes sense."

It did not make sense, and I now regretted that I had joined him at his table and wasted some of my precious lunch time talking to him. He was a bona fide kook. It was a mistake to think he might know something. I looked around the room to see if any other tables had opened up where I could finish my lunch in peace. Unfortunately no. The place was still packed. I might as well continue eating my salad and soup where I was. The sooner I finished, the sooner I could leave.

"Think about it," he said, leaning forward. "*Astronomy.* And then suddenly feds are on the scene and it's all very hush-hush."

No doubt he believed Area 51 in Nevada was concealing the remains of a flying saucer and maybe a dead alien or two.

"So you think feds killed Mr. Malinsky?" I asked in a carefully neutral voice. "Or are you suggesting aliens killed him?" *Eat faster*, I told myself.

"No, of course not." He looked offended. "Why would you say that? That's crazy."

"Feds then."

"Yes. Of course."

"But why?"

"To keep us from knowing the truth."

"And what's that?"

"That we're in contact with aliens." He said it as if it should be obvious.

I rolled my eyes. I should have seen that coming. How could this conversation get any nuttier?

"Don't tell me you don't believe there's life out there in the universe?" he demanded.

"I do. Out there. Not *here*. And it may not be anything like us. In fact, it's probably not anything like us." My grandfather had believed there was life out there *somewhere*. Intelligent life, not just bacteria. But it was probably too faraway for us to ever make contact.

"Or maybe it's exactly like us," Kevin said. "Maybe they're here right now."

He had watched too many sci-fi movies. Or too many old episodes of *Star Trek*. I sighed.

"Why do you think you're being followed?" I asked.

"I've seen them."

"What do they look like?"

"Feds."

I nearly choked on a spoonful of clam chowder. It was not what I was expecting. I thought of Barb's man in black.

"Why would they be following you?" I asked when I could speak again.

"To stop me from telling what I know." He sounded as if he really believed that. A true conspiracy buff.

I glanced at my watch. Time to leave if I didn't want to be late for my next class, but first I had one more question for him. "Were you following me the other day when I saw you at Starbucks at the mall?"

He looked taken aback. "Of course not. I go there all the time."

I started to rise and he grabbed my arm.

"Who was that guy you were with—your boyfriend?"

"Maybe." I pulled my arm free and headed toward the door. My personal life was my business. Just because we had talked didn't mean I had to share my life with him.

CHAPTER 13

Of course, I didn't believe Kevin Burke and his wild theory about feds and aliens. I suspected he had gone to Mr. Malinsky's apartment building to find out what he could about the murder and had stumbled upon Barb, who had told him about the man in black, just as she had told me. It had fed his paranoia and conspiracy theories. The man she had seen might not even have been the killer. But could he have been the same man who showed up at Mrs. Calhoun's office asking questions about me? That was what I would have liked to know.

So Kevin was not the only one feeling paranoid. My own fears kept coming back to my mother's box. I worried that someone might try to steal it, and so now I carried it with me everywhere I went. Maybe I should have taken it back to the bank and stashed it in a safe deposit box again, but I liked being able to take it out and look at it and touch it whenever I felt like it. I couldn't help feeling it might be the key to everything. Maybe it had nothing to do with Mr. Malinsky's death, but what if it did? Suppose someone had found out that he had the key to my grandfather's safe deposit box and had killed him trying to find out where the key was or where the box was. Maybe the box was valuable and someone knew that. Undeniably it was a beautiful and mysterious object. I still didn't know what it was or what was in it, and I couldn't make up my mind to open it, although a dozen times a day I considered doing exactly that.

When my classes were done for the day and I was on my way home, I was still mulling over what I had learned from Mrs. Calhoun and my weird conversation with Kevin Burke. But when I got home and started to unlock my door, I was jolted back to the present moment. My door was unlocked. Again. I stared at it in disbelief. Ever since the break-in I had been extra careful to lock it.

I hesitated, my hand on the doorknob. Someone could be inside. I should not take chances and walk into a dangerous situation. I took out my cell phone to call 911, then stood there debating what to do. Suppose no one was inside. The police would be annoyed that I had wasted their time. They would think I was overreacting. Or that I wanted attention. And what if they didn't believe me when I told them I hadn't left the door unlocked? I didn't want to be like the boy who cried wolf. When I really needed them, they might not show up.

So steeling myself, I pushed the door open. My heart was pounding. "I'm home," I called out, hoping my voice didn't shake. No answer. No sound of movement. My eyes flew around the room. Nothing out of place. Everything looked normal. I forced myself to step inside, set down my violin case and pocketbook, and slip my backpack off my back. I moved cautiously from room to room—living room, kitchen, bedroom, bathroom. I opened the closet door. No sign of an intruder anywhere. In relief I sank down on a kitchen chair, knees weak, hands trembling, and speed dialed Matt. When he didn't pick up, I texted him.

"Maybe you were wrong about the door being locked," Matt said later when he came over after work and examined the lock.

Outside it had begun to rain.

I was beginning to wonder myself if I could have been wrong. If there had been an intruder, why hadn't my apartment been trashed again? Was it the same intruder or a different one? Yeah, right, a *nicer* intruder, a small sarcastic voice in my head muttered.

"Do you still think it was someone after the box?" I asked him. It was sitting on the table again with the hanging lamp throwing a circle of warm yellow light around it. I had taken it out of my backpack to look at it.

Matt left the door and came to stand beside me, looking at the box. "I think this whole business has been upsetting for you. Your father's death. Malinsky's murder. The break-in."

"What about what Mrs. Calhoun said—that someone was asking questions about me?"

He shrugged and put his arms around me. "Maybe it had nothing to do with the box. Look, why not just open it and find out what's in it? Put your mind to rest once and for all."

I bit my lip and didn't answer. Maybe what was in the box was something so awful I wouldn't want to know about it. Or maybe it was empty. That would almost be worse. I wanted it to contain information about my mother's mysterious past. As long as I didn't open it, I could hope that it held answers about her. I needed answers.

"Or take it back to the bank."

Then I might never know what was in it. No, I didn't want to take it back to the bank.

"If it would make you feel better, I could take it home with me."

I considered this. It would mean I didn't have to worry about someone stealing it, but was it any safer with Matt? Surely a determined thief could break into his apartment as easily as into mine? And if someone had figured out the box was in my possession, couldn't they figure out it was in his? I trusted him, but I felt uncomfortable letting the box out of my sight. Besides a few photographs, it was all I had left of my mother. As my grandfather had said, it was my legacy.

"If someone is trying to get their hands on the box, it might not be that safe to carry it around with you." His lips brushed my hair.

He was right, but I didn't want to give up the box. I would take the risk.

"Maybe there's no connection to the murder of Mr. Malinsky," I said.

A kiss on the side of my neck. "I don't think you believe that."

He was right. I didn't. But I wasn't going to part with the box. I pulled back and lifted my chin. "I'll be careful."

He sighed. "Anybody ever tell you you're stubborn?"

"My grandfather. He said it runs in the family."

* * *

Although I thought I was handling the loss of my grandfather well, maybe I wasn't handling it as well as I thought. That realization struck me the next day when I had a rougher than usual session with Mr. Hajek, my violin instructor. Mr. Hajek, who was in his fifties, came from Prague and still spoke with a thick accent although he had been in the country for years. After more than a year of working with him, I was used to his occasional outbursts of temper. After all, most violinists who have played professionally are temperamental. It goes with the territory. I understood that. So when I launched into the Beethoven sonata I had been working on for weeks and he stopped me almost immediately, I did not take it personally.

"No, no, no. You are *butchering* it," he said, waving his arms melodramatically. He was a man of feeling, both when he liked something and when he found fault with something. "Beethoven would be *horrified* if he heard you. He would turn in his grave. This is not how he should sound. You play like a first-year student."

I accepted the criticism stoically. I knew I wasn't playing my best. Maybe I had not been getting enough sleep. Maybe I had too much on my mind. My grandfather. Matt. The death of Mr. Malinsky.

"This is not like you. What's wrong? Is something bothering you?"

"It's been a hard week." I wasn't sure if he knew about my grandfather dying, but I was determined not to use his death as an excuse.

Mr. Hajek ran his hand through his greying hair. He was an imposing man, tall, thick-bodied, with a grizzled beard. When he was angry, he reminded me of a bear.

"That should make no difference. Do you think a professional violinist tells his audience, 'Excuse me, I'm not playing well today because I've had a hard week'? Of course not. He goes out on the stage and gives his audience his best because that's what they expect. That's what they have paid for. They don't care about your problems."

I waited for his fit of temper to pass, as I knew it would.

He started to pace. "If you want to be a professional, you must learn to focus. You must put everything else out of your mind. There is only you and the music. Never forget that."

How many times had he told me this? I was sorry to have disappointed him and vowed to do better next time.

He shook his head. "What would your mother say if she heard you play like this?"

My mother? For a moment I thought I had misheard. He had never mentioned my mother before. I didn't know he knew anything about her. But his next comment told me he did.

"They say she could make audiences weep when she played her violin. What would she think if she heard you play so badly?"

I was surprised that he had brought up my mother. My grandfather had always said she was very talented and could have played professionally. But her death at twenty-five had prevented that. *I* had prevented that. Who remembered my mother today? How had Mr. Hajak even heard of her? Then a thought struck me.

"Did you ever hear her play?" I asked, wondering if he might have heard her *before* my father met her. If he had, maybe he would know something about her past.

He had calmed down now. "No, but I've heard of her. People say she had great promise. If she had gone on, she might have been one of the greats of her generation."

"She died when I was born."

"A great loss—for you and for the world."

"I wish I could have known her."

He sighed. "Such is life. We have no idea how much time we have. And that's why you must learn how to focus. I have told you before. You will never be a great violinist unless you can put everything else aside and focus on your music. The violin must be everything. It is all that matters."

"Shall I try it again?"

He paced some more, scowling. He seemed so lost in thought that I wasn't sure he had heard me. "You have much promise, like your mother. But if you can't focus . . ."

There it was. My mother again. Why was she on his mind today?

"They say she was exceptional. One in a thousand."

"Who told you this?" I asked.

He frowned. "It's not important."

"It is to me. I never knew her."

He looked surprised that I had challenged him. Usually I was the docile student who quietly endured his rants, as was expected. He hesitated a long minute, then said, "Professor Merrick told me about her."

"Who?" I didn't recognize the name.

He sighed. "Professor Merrick. He was chair of the music department when your mother was here. A very talented musician himself and an old friend."

I felt disappointed. "He's not here anymore."

"Not at the university, no, but he's still in the area. Still very much alive. Sometimes I go see him. He's in Sunnyside Manor, where old musicians go to die." He shook his head and passed a hand across his eyes. "Perhaps I will go there myself one day."

I filed away what I had just learned. There were so few people who had known my mother that the possibility of finding someone who had excited me. Maybe he would even be able to clear up some of the mystery about where she came from. I resolved then and there to track down Professor Merrick and find out what he could tell me about my mother.

CHAPTER 14

A few days earlier I had received a notice that unless I paid an additional month's rent, my grandfather's apartment would be opened to would-be renters by the end of the month. I could delay no longer the task of packing up my grandfather's belongings. Matt volunteered to help me and on Saturday showed up with TJ and Joy and his trunk full of boxes. We spent the afternoon boxing up the rest of my grandfather's possessions. Matt and TJ worked on the kitchen and living room while Joy and I tackled the bedrooms.

"God, I'm going to miss him," I said, picking up the small lamp that had stood on the nightstand by his bed for as long as I could remember. "My grandfather was all I had. I barely remember my dad. And I never knew my mom. In fact, I know almost nothing about her—except that she played the violin."

"I lost my dad when I was twelve," Joy said, folding the sheet she had just removed from the bed. "For a while all I wanted to do at school was get in fights, and I mean real fights. The knock-down, make-'em squeal-in-pain type. Didn't matter if they were bigger than me. In fact, the bigger, the better."

"Did it take you long to get past that?"

"Just until I got into a fight that left me with some broken ribs. You try fighting with broken ribs." She shook her head.

I smiled. I could imagine her beating up one of her classmates when she was twelve. She was a born fighter.

"Are you and TJ an item now?" I asked.

She cocked her head and narrowed her eyes. "I haven't decided. He can be a jerk at times. What about you and Matt?"

"I guess so."

"You don't sound too certain."

"Well, I have plans to go to Juilliard in the spring."

"Let me guess. You're not sure how Matt fits into those plans."

"Well, yes."

"You talked to him about it?"

"Sort of."

"What did he say?"

"He doesn't want me to go."

"But you do."

"Yeah."

"So go and see what happens. Anyway that's months away. In the meantime you have a chance to find out how you feel about each other."

"I'm not sure that's fair to him."

"What's not fair? He's a big boy. He can take care of himself."

"But I shouldn't—"

"Listen, my mama always says worry about today's problems today, and let tomorrow's problems wait for tomorrow."

I sighed. She was right. Maybe I should stop worrying about the future. But I didn't want to end up somewhere I didn't want to be in five or ten years. As Mr. Hajek so frequently reminded me, my violin needed to be my top priority. I mustn't let myself get distracted, and Matt was definitely a distraction, but one I wasn't sure I wanted to get rid of. I packed the lamp in a box with wadded up newspaper to cushion it. Then I bent down to look under the bed to see if anything was there. I spotted a shoebox and pulled it out. It was battered and dusty. An old pair of shoes my grandfather had forgotten about?

"What's that?" Joy asked.

"I'm not sure." I lifted off the lid. "Oh."

There were old photographs in the box, at least a dozen of them. I spread them out on the bed, my excitement growing. I didn't remember ever seeing these before. One showed my mother holding her violin beneath her chin, bow raised, as if ready to play, a look of concentration on her face. Others were of her and my father. They looked so young! In one my father had his arms around my mother, both looking so happy and in love. In the background red rocks jutted up against the sky. But that wasn't all. As I looked closer, I spotted the box on a boulder behind them. Only a sliver of it was visible, but I recognized it at once. It caught the light of the sun and reflected it back at the camera. I felt as if I had stumbled across the Rosetta stone. Here were all three pieces of the puzzle together: my parents, the red rocks, and the box.

"I've got to show this to Matt," I said, snatching up the photo.

He and TJ were in the living room packing up my grandfather's books. The bookcase shelves looked strangely bare with the books missing.

"Look," I said, waving the photo. "There's the box."

Matt studied the photo. "Maybe. It could just be the light reflecting off something."

"No, it's the box. I'm sure of it."

"That's your mom and dad?"

"Yes."

"Where'd you find it?"

"Under his bed in a shoebox."

He turned the photo over and looked at the back. It was blank. "Anything there that would explain what it is?"

"No. Just other photos."

Joy, who had followed me into the room, noticed my backpack sitting on the floor beside the desk and nudged it with the toe of her sneaker. "What's this?"

"Oh, that's mine," I said. "That's—"

"That's the mysterious box left for her by her mother," Matt said.

"What's mysterious about it?"

"She doesn't know what's in it."

"Why not?"

He looked at me.

"My grandfather didn't think I should open it."

"Why don't you show it to them?" Matt said.

Joy and TJ had just helped pack up my grandfather's belongings. How could I refuse to let them see it? I hesitated for a fraction of a second, then reached for my backpack, unzipped it, and took out the box. It caught the light streaming in through the window and seemed to glow.

"Oh, you got to open that," TJ said.

"Someone's trying to get their hands on it," Matt said.

"Maybe," I added quickly. "We can't be sure."

"Your mother left you that?" Joy said. "And she didn't give you any hint what's inside?"

"I'm not sure she intended for me to have it. It was actually my grandfather who left it for me."

"I saw a movie about a box once," TJ said. "Everybody who opened it had all kinds of bad things happen to them."

Joy rolled her eyes. "Maybe it's a biological weapon."

TJ gave her a look. "Seriously?"

"Whatever it is," Matt said, "someone may be willing to kill to get their hands on it."

"How do you figure that?" Joy asked.

"The man who had the key to the safe deposit box where her grandfather was keeping this got his throat slit the same day he gave Lauren the key."

"You're kidding, right?"

"Nope."

I looked again at the photo of my mother and father with the red rocks in the background and the flash of light where the edge of the box was visible. Why had the box been in that photo? What was I missing? Somewhere there were answers. But where?

"Maybe there's something in the box that would explain," Matt suggested later that afternoon after we had carried the boxes of my grandfather's things into my apartment and stacked them against the wall in the living room. I had no idea what I was going to do with them. I would have to sort through them and see what to save, what to donate, and what to discard. His furniture would be donated to Goodwill.

"Maybe," I agreed, glancing at my mother's box, which was sitting in the middle of the table again. If only she had left a letter explaining what it was. But of course she hadn't known she would die giving birth to me.

"You okay?" Matt asked.

"Yeah, just thinking."

"Don't think so hard." He kissed me on the forehead. "Listen, are you doing anything Sunday? My mom said to invite you for dinner."

"Why?" I felt a twinge of alarm.

"She wants to meet you."

"She does?" That didn't make me feel any less anxious. Introducing me to his family seemed like a big step in our relationship. I wasn't sure I was ready for it.

"Don't look so scared. She'll love you. The rest of the family too."

"But—" How to explain? It was too soon, too serious. *Take a deep breath*, I told myself. *It's only dinner, not the rest of your life.* But I couldn't help thinking of my parents, who had leaped into marriage just ten days after meeting each other. I didn't want the same thing to happen to us.

CHAPTER 15

On Sunday afternoon I drove to Sunnyside Manor, an assisted living facility on the north side of the city. It was a well-kept building which looked like a resort hotel located on an expanse of lawn shaded by several large maple trees, their leaves now red with autumn plumage. The woman at the front desk directed me to the solarium, a spacious room with floor-to-ceiling windows looking out on a garden. Mr. Merrick was sitting in a wheelchair facing the garden when I entered the room. He was a fragile-looking elderly man with wispy white flyaway hair and thick-lensed glasses He sat alone in the room, listening to Mozart's Symphony No. 40 in G minor issuing from two small white speakers. I told him who I was and asked if he remembered my mother.

"Of course, I remember her," he said. "One of the most gifted violinists I've ever heard. It was like she could hear and play notes no one else could. She should have been performing in Paris and Vienna. Such a gift!"

"Did you know her well?"

"No, I wouldn't say well. She was only with us for a short time. But she was a lovely woman. You remind me of her. You have her eyes."

No one had ever told me that before. I wondered if it was true.

"Do you remember anything about her background?" I asked. "She died when I was born, and I know very little about her. Practically nothing."

He puckered his forehead, concentrating. "There was something odd about her background if I remember correctly. What was it? A fire that destroyed records or something like that. But once I heard her play, I had no reservations about hiring her. We were lucky to have her. She was a true virtuoso."

"Do you know if she was from Canada?"

He frowned. "Sorry, my dear. It's so long ago. I don't remember. She might have been." He paused. "Listen. This is my favorite part."

We sat for a few minutes in silence listening to the bright and impetuous music of Mozart's Great G minor Symphony. I looked out at the garden and the fall foliage. It was a beautiful view and the music seemed made for it. I felt a wave of happiness wash over me.

"He was only thirty-five when he died," Mr. Merrick said. "Can you imagine what he might have been able to write if he had lived longer?" Mr. Merrick shook his head. "So much music to squeeze into so little time. And so much life too. The older I grow, the more I admire him for what he did with the time he had."

I thought of my mother, who had also had so little time.

"What about you, dear? Do you play the violin too?"

"Yes, I do."

"That's good. I'm sure your mother would be pleased."

I looked at his hands resting on the arms of his wheelchair, mottled and bony with ropy blue veins. "What instrument did you play?"

He chuckled. "What didn't I? Piano, cello, harp, flute—you name it."

"A Renaissance man."

"Ha, I like that."

When the music ended, I stood to leave, not wanting to tire him.

"What is your name again?" he asked.

"Lauren."

He nodded. "You look so much like her."

I doubted that. I had seen photographs of my mother. She was a beautiful woman. I looked very little like her.

"Leaving so soon? You should come visit me again. Bring your violin and play for me. I would love to hear you play."

I promised him I would do that.

Matt's family lived in an older residential section of the city made up of two-story houses which had seen better days. They had porches where people could sit outside on a hot summer night on a swing and maple trees which were starting to lose their leaves. Yellow light spilled from the windows in the gathering dusk. When we climbed out of Matt's car, I noticed the cracks in the sidewalk and the tufts of grass sprouting up through the cracks. An old red tricycle stood overturned by the front steps.

Matt squeezed my hand. "You okay?"

"Yes." I wasn't sure why I was so nervous. I think I was afraid I would disappoint them.

We had just stepped into the house when a little boy came barreling out of the living room and careened into Matt's legs.

"They're here!" he shouted.

"This is Davey," Matt said, tousling the boy's hair.

A girl of about ten with a head of unruly black curls and an impish grin appeared next. She twisted her arms in front of her self-consciously. "Hi. I'm Felicia."

Then a strapping teenaged boy came bounding down the narrow stairway beside us. He barely glanced at me. "The Rat's home," he shouted.

"The Rat?"

"Don't ask."

Matt's mother appeared a moment later in the doorway, wiping her hands on a tea towel. Her brown hair streaked with grey was slipping loose in wisps from the band which held it back. She gave me a warm smile and shook my hand. "You must be Lauren. We've heard so much about you."

I glanced at Matt, wondering what he had told his family about me.

"So sorry about your grandfather," she added quickly.

Matt's father stepped out of the living room, and Matt introduced me to him. He had hair greying at the temples and smile lines around his eyes. He wore a grey work shirt with a company logo on the pocket. He too shook my hand.

"So you're Lauren," he said in a way that made me wonder again what Matt had told them about me. I had the distinct impression I was being checked out, and that made me feel even more nervous.

"I guess we're ready," Matt's mother said. "We were just waiting for you. We're so glad you could join us, Lauren."

Soon we were seated around a table covered by a cheerful flowered tablecloth and laid with white plates, glasses of water, silverware, a platter of beef, and several colorful bowls of vegetables. The family said grace. Then dishes began to pass, and we filled our plates. Of course, I had eaten at friends' houses before, but in situations like this I never quite got over the feeling of being a visitor from another country. Every family seemed to have its own set of rules about whether or not you could grab for food or talk with your mouth full and what topics were taboo. For the first few minutes Matt's mother tried to maintain order, but then she sighed and seemed to resign herself to letting her family do as they pleased. Davey used his fingers more than was generally considered polite. Warren tried his best to shock his parents or nettle Matt when he wasn't shoveling food into his mouth. Felicia, on the other hand, was fastidious about her eating habits. I noticed she was taking pains to separate her peas and carrots from the potatoes and beef so that each item occupied its own space on her plate.

I wondered what it was like to grow up in a large family like Matt's. His oldest brother and married sister had once been part of this brood. Six children. I stole glances at his mother. Matt had told me she worked as a bookkeeper for a small accounting firm. She not only had a job but managed a house and a large family too. No mean feat.

"So why'd you and Sherry break up?" the older boy, Warren, asked. He was sitting across the table from us next to little Davey.

His mother shot him a warning look.

"Watch it," his father said. "What did I tell you?"

"What?" Warren said.

"So Matt says you're studying at the university, Lauren," his father said. "What are you going to do after you graduate?"

I glanced at Matt. "Well, actually I'm transferring to Juilliard next spring. I'm majoring in music. I play the violin."

He looked at me as if I had just sprouted a second head. Evidently Matt hadn't told him I played the violin.

"Violin?" his mother said. "How nice. I played flute in my high school band."

"What do your folks think about that?" his father asked.

I hesitated, wondering how to answer without saying, *they're dead*. Davey was watching me with interest, a green bean held between his fingers as if he were trying to decide what to do with it. Even Felicia and Warren seemed to pause as if they sensed I was about to trip up.

"She's an orphan," Matt's mother said in a low voice. "She was raised by her grandfather, who just died."

"Who died?" Davey asked.

"Sorry," said Matt's father.

"Sherry was studying cosmetology at the community college," Warren said. "She's got her own salon now."

"One more word about Sherry and you can go to your room," his mother said.

"Sorry," Matt muttered under his breath.

I was glad when the meal was done. I helped carry dishes from the table to the kitchen. "How do you make your hair wave like that?" Felicia asked, shadowing me.

"It waves all by itself."

She sighed. "I wish mine did that."

"You have very pretty hair," her mother said. "When you're a little older, you'll be grateful you have such beautiful curls."

Felicia groaned and rolled her eyes.

Her mother turned to me and smiled. "I think it's wonderful that you play the violin, Lauren. If that's what you want to do, don't let anybody stop you."

I wondered if someone had stopped her from doing something she wanted to do, but I didn't know her well enough to ask.

"Mom?" Matt stood in the doorway. "Do you mind if we run? I've got an early shift tomorrow."

"You're leaving already?" She looked disappointed.

"The dishes . . ." I said, looking at the plates, silverware, and glasses crowding the counter.

She waved a hand dismissively. "Leave them. Felicia will help me."

Matt gave her a quick hug.

"Everything okay at work?" she asked in a low voice.

"Of course."

"I know this is what you want to do, but . . ."

"You just told Lauren not to let anything stop her. I heard you."

"Chasing bad guys with guns is not the same thing."

"Sure it is." He gave her a peck on the cheek. "You worry too much."

Moments later we were walking across the grass to his car.

"What'd you think?" he asked. "Sorry about Warren. And my dad."

"No, they were great."

"Thank you for doing this for me."

"Should I worry about Sherry?"

"Nah. Warren's just trying to get under my skin. I was probably just as obnoxious at his age."

"Did I pass inspection?"

"With flying colors." He grinned.

"You don't think your dad . . . ?"

"If he disapproves of anyone, it's me because I didn't want to be a plumber."

He pulled me close and we kissed. Whenever we kissed, my doubts slipped away, and I let myself sink into a sort of mindless bliss. But when the kiss ended, my doubts returned.

"Joanne wants to meet you too," Matt said when we were in his car.

"Joanne?"

"My older sister."

"Oh."

"What's the matter. Why so quiet?"

I couldn't tell him the truth—that I didn't think I could be what he wanted me to be. He would be hurt. And how could I explain so he would understand? It wasn't just because of what happened to my mother and father, their lives cut tragically short, although that was part of it. No, it was because I had wanted to play the violin for as long as I could remember. I couldn't give it up like his mother had given up the flute. My violin—my music—was as necessary to me as the air I breathed.

CHAPTER 16

I was driving home after classes the next day, listening to my car radio, when news came on of a hostage situation in progress. Police had responded to a domestic violence call, and it had escalated into a standoff. A woman's ex-husband was holding her and their two young children hostage. Shots had been fired. An officer was down.

I felt as if a fist had reached out and gripped my heart and was squeezing. I tried to tell myself Matt was nowhere near the hostage crisis. He had probably been giving out speeding tickets on the other side of the city. But all the same I felt icy shivers of fear run up and down my spine. What if it was Matt who had been shot? What if he was bleeding to death at that very moment or—even worse—already dead? The rest of the ride passed in a tumult of anxious thoughts. It's a wonder I didn't have an accident.

As soon as I pulled up to the curb outside my apartment house, I texted him. Then I hurried inside and searched on the internet to see if I could find any updates. But there was nothing more than what I had already heard on the radio. I wished I knew someone to call who might know if he was safe—TJ or Matt's parents, his older brother, or his married sister. But I had no phone numbers for any of them.

I turned on TV to catch the evening news as I warmed up leftovers for dinner. I didn't feel like cooking or eating. I just wanted to know that Matt was safe. But all I learned from the TV news was that the standoff was still in progress and the wounded policeman was in critical condition. *It's not him*, I told myself again, *and if it is, at least he's not dead.*

I tried to work on my Prokofiev paper, but it was impossible. I couldn't think about anything else. Why didn't Matt text or call? I had left three messages for him.

It was past seven when he finally phoned. I felt so relieved at the sound of his voice that I almost sobbed. He told me, yes, he had been there at the hostage crisis. One of the other officers had been shot and was in the hospital, now in stable condition. Could he come over later when he got off?

It was after nine when he arrived, still in his uniform. I threw my arms around his neck.

"Thank god you're okay."

"Of course, I'm okay," he said. "I'm the man of steel. Or Teflon. Or something like that. Bullets bounce off me."

"You could have been killed."

He stretched out his arms, grinning. "But I wasn't. See. Here I am. Alive and in one piece."

He didn't seem to understand how close to danger he had come. I had been scared out of my wits, and he was joking about it?

"Weren't you scared?"

"I didn't have time to be scared. I was scared afterward when it was all over. I thought I was going to throw up. First time jitters they said."

"You seem very hyper."

"It's adrenaline. I feel like I could jump off a cliff and survive. I feel like Superman."

"You're not Superman. You could have been shot."

"Yeah, I know." He was still grinning. "Hey, want to go somewhere?"

I didn't. I was a wreck after all those hours of worry and not knowing if he was hurt. "It's late. I have school tomorrow."

"We could have a beer. Or a cup of coffee."

I shook my head. "Coffee will keep me awake."

He put his arms around me again. "What's the matter?"

I pulled away. "Nothing."

"It's something. Come on, tell me. What's wrong?"

"I thought you were hurt."

"Nope."

"I thought you might be dead."

"Hey, I'm all right. I'm right here."

I felt like something inside me was about to snap. "I can't do this." The words slipped out before I could stop them. I suppose it was the culmination of all the fear that had been building inside me since I first heard the news of the hostage situation on my car radio that afternoon. It was like a scream that I had been stifling.

"Can't do what?"

Now that I had said it, the floodgates were open. I didn't think I could hold my feelings back. "This isn't going to work."

"What do you mean?"

"Just that. It's not going to work."

He went very still. "You don't mean that."

"I do."

"You're upset."

"I can't lose anyone else."

My words seemed to hang in the air between us.

"You're not going to lose me."

"You can't know that."

"It's no reason to break up."

Wasn't it? Wasn't it just as good a reason as any other? Maybe better?

"We don't belong together," I said. "Can't you see that? We're too different. I'm going to go to Juilliard in the spring. You're going to be here. And there will be other hostage crises and armed robberies and carjackings and . . . I can't do it."

He reached toward me, but I moved away because if he touched me I would be lost. Couldn't he see that it wasn't going to work out? We came from different backgrounds. We wanted different things. It was never going to work out. Better to break up now. He would get over it. We would both get over it. Sometimes relationships don't work out. This was one of those times.

"Was it something I said?"

"Please, just go." I couldn't look at him. I couldn't bear to see the hurt on his face.

A minute later I heard the door close behind him. Then I began to cry.

CHAPTER 17

I didn't really want to get out of bed the next day, but I knew I had to. I forced myself to get up and go to classes even though I didn't feel like it. I looked forward to the afternoon, when I would have time to lose myself in practice. I thought I would find comfort in my violin, but for once it failed me. I couldn't concentrate. I kept thinking about Matt. If only my grandfather had still been around to talk to. I felt so confused and unhappy. All my life my violin was all that had really mattered to me. Other girls obsessed over boyfriends and falling in love; I only cared about my violin and the music I could coax from it. Now for the first time in my life I wondered if it was enough. Would being a violinist satisfy me ten years from now? I didn't know.

As I pondered this question, I thought of Sheila, expecting her first child. I wondered if she worried about how being a mother would impact her career. She always looked like she was in complete control of her life. No meltdowns like I had just gone through. Would being a mother mean she had to give up the violin, and if it did, could she?

The more I thought about it, the more I wanted to ask her. Finally I decided to call her, but when she answered I realized it wasn't something I could ask on the phone. I wanted to talk to her in person.

"Of course, come on over," she said. "Jeff's watching a documentary on TV—the Byzantine empire or something equally exciting. I won't have to talk to myself."

When I showed up at her door a half hour later, her husband answered. He was tall and wore glasses, which he was in the habit of pushing higher on the bridge of his nose. He taught world history at the university.

"Hi, Lauren," he said, showing no surprise to see me. "Sheila's in the kitchen."

I had been to their house before and knew my way, so he returned to his TV documentary.

Sheila was putting a tray of muffins in the oven when I found her. She looked the picture of domesticity in her neat and orderly kitchen where everything seemed to be in its appointed place.

"What's up?" she asked. "You sounded a tad desperate on the phone."

Now that I was there, I felt embarrassed. Did I really want to tell her I'd broken up with Matt? I wasn't sure she even knew I was dating him.

"When's the baby due?" I asked, stalling.

"December."

She was definitely showing, impossible not to notice that bulge beneath her smock.

"I guess you'll have to take a break from the orchestra."

She tilted her head to the side, considering. "There's no reason I can't play until close to my due date."

"But afterward . . ." Surely having a baby would make a difference?

"We'll see. I don't really want to give up the orchestra. I'd be miserable. Jeff agrees."

"Did you ever feel you had to choose . . . ?"

"You mean, between having a career and my marriage?"

"Well, yes."

She scrunched up her face, considering, then relaxed into a smile. "I think I always knew I wanted to be someone's wife."

"You never wanted to be a world class violinist?" This surprised me because she was good.

She shook her head. "Not if it means giving up a chance for a normal life."

"I wish I could be that certain."

"What's this all about?"

I sighed. "I just broke up with my boyfriend."

"That cute guy who came to our last concert?"

She had noticed? "Yes—that would be the one."

"Why does it have to be one or the other?"

She didn't seem to see the conflict. I tried to explain.

"If I go to Juilliard in the spring and he stays here . . . And later I would have to travel . . . Mr. Hajek says I need to decide what really matters."

"Does he?" She rolled her eyes. "He's married, you know. Being married didn't stop *him*."

"It's different for a woman."

She arched an eyebrow. "Is it?"

* * *

Certainly part of me agreed with her. There shouldn't be any difference between men and women violin virtuosos. But everyone assumed a man could put his talent before all else, whereas a woman would be considered selfish if she did so. The only way she could do it was if she didn't choose to have a family. It wasn't fair, but that's the way it was. If I wanted to be a violin virtuoso, I might as well accept that.

I drove home, intending to spend the evening working on the Prokofiev paper. I was barely in my apartment before my cell phone rang. I picked up quickly, thinking it might be Matt. But there was just silence. In the next hour my phone rang several more times. Each time I answered it, it either sounded dead or there was an odd ringing tone followed by disconnection. I wondered if pranksters were deliberately targeting my number. I tried phoning Joy, but I just got the odd ringing tone. I'd have to take my phone to the service center tomorrow and see if they could fix the problem. In the meantime I needed to finish the paper on Prokofiev. The deadline was looming.

I decided I might accomplish more if I went to the library, and so after a light dinner, I set off with my laptop. I took my violin and the box with me in case there was another break-in. I figured they were safer with me. The box in my backpack, safely out of sight, and my violin in its case.

As I walked from the parking garage to the library, it began to rain. At the same time there was a chill in the air that made me wonder if maybe I should have stayed home after all. But since I had come this far, I thought I might as well continue on. At least I had my umbrella with me.

The campus library wasn't crowded. Maybe the chilly weather and rain were keeping students away. After finding the books I needed, I settled down at a table to get some work done. For the next hour or so I made good progress. Not until the lights blinked off and on to warn closing time was approaching did I realize it was already eight-thirty. I looked around the room and was surprised to see I was one of the few students remaining. That's when I noticed a man in a black suit and tie standing near the checkout desk. He looked out of place. Not even teachers wore suits and ties. He was too old to be a student, and he certainly didn't look like a librarian.

Then our eyes met and locked. I had the uncomfortable feeling that he had been watching me. A disturbing thought occurred to me. Could he be Barb's man in black? I knew I shouldn't jump to conclusions. Most likely he was an administrator or staff or undercover security.

Without looking at him, I gathered up my things. I rummaged in my purse for my phone, then remembered it wasn't working. Who would I call anyway—campus security? What would I tell them?

I left the library books I had been using on the table and started walking toward the exit. I studied the man as I got closer, but he turned his back and ignored me. Relieved, I passed through the turnstile. When I got outside, it was still raining. I put up my umbrella and headed toward the parking garage.

Before long I heard footsteps and looked back. The man from the library was following me. I broke into a run, which wasn't easy carrying an umbrella, my pocketbook, backpack, and violin case. Why had I stayed at the library so late? And why wasn't the campus better lighted? With the rain coming down, visibility was poor. I collapsed the umbrella so I could run faster, never mind the rain.

As I sprinted into the parking garage, my pursuer was gaining on me. There was no doubt now that I was his quarry. A car that was leaving barely missed me, then slammed on its brakes for the man behind me. When I glanced back, I saw him caught in its headlights, a startled look on his face before he resumed the chase. It gave me just enough time to jump in my car and lock the doors.

He looked at me through my windshield, a sneer on his face, as if he thought he had me cornered, but I started the engine and he sprang aside with a curse as I floored the accelerator. At first I drove fast, not caring if the police stopped me. Gradually I calmed down, certain that I had given him the slip. The car wipers flicked back and forth, a comforting rhythm. My first instinct was to head home, but then I realized that would be the first place he looked for me. Almost certainly he knew where I lived. I had no idea who he was, but if he had murdered Mr. Malinsky, I didn't want to be his next victim. I would have to find someplace else to go. But where?

Was any place safe now? I wished I could talk to Matt. He would know what to do. But I didn't want to put him in danger—or his family. The same was true for his friends. Or mine. I couldn't expect anyone to take the risk. Maybe the best thing was for me to leave—to just disappear for a while. But where could I go? Who would hide me?

Suddenly there flashed through my mind the photograph of my mother and father standing in front of the red rocks, the edge of the box just a sliver of light behind them. Somehow that image seemed to me like the answer to everything. A crazy plan began to form in my head. I could go to where it all began. Aunt Nora had said my parents met in the town of Sedona in Arizona. Why not go there and see what I could find out? Maybe someone would remember them. Or maybe someone would know about the box. At the very least, it would give me a place to go, and no one would think to look for me there. The more I thought about it, the more I liked this plan.

I was glad now that I had brought my violin and the box with me. I would not have to risk going back to my apartment for them. But I should find a way to let Matt know where I was going. We had broken up, but I didn't want him to worry, and he would if I just disappeared.

I couldn't phone him since my cell phone wasn't working, but I did know a way I could get a message to him.

It was late when I pulled into the mall parking lot, almost closing time. I was pretty sure I hadn't been followed. I entered the mall close on the heels of a group of high school students, trying to blend in. Once inside, I headed straight for the Apple store.

I was in luck. TJ was still there. I stood just outside the store and waited until he was done helping a teenaged boy decide on a phone.

He looked up in surprise when I approached. I wondered how many security cameras were focused on us. Well, nothing I could do about that.

"Lauren. What's up?"

"I wonder if you could give Matt a message for me."

"Why not give it to him yourself?"

I hesitated. "My phone's not working."

He looked at me skeptically. "Did you two have a fight?"

Evidently Matt had not told him we broke up.

"Something like that. Look, I have to go away for a while. Can you tell him I'll explain when I get back?"

"Where are you going?"

"I can't tell you that."

"Why not?"

"I just can't."

"When are you coming back?"

"I don't know. Look, I just need some time to think." I glanced back at the doorway, half expecting to see the man in black standing there.

TJ noticed. "Are you in some kind of trouble?"

"No, of course not."

He didn't look convinced. "Why don't you call Matt and tell him?"

"I told you. I can't. My phone's not working."

"You can use my phone." He pulled his out and laid it on the table between us.

"Please, TJ—"

"Are you telling the truth? Is your phone really not working?"

"Yes."

He looked around. There were only a few stragglers in the store now and half a dozen young black-shirted salesmen, one of whom was watching us intently.

"Look, do you need money or anything?"

I shook my head.

"If you *are* in trouble,"—he held up a hand to stop me as I started to protest—"I'm just saying, if you *are*, you might want to ditch your phone—whether it's working or not. It can be used to track you, you know."

I glanced up at a security camera pointed down at us. He was right. Maybe they were already tracking me. Maybe they knew exactly where I was. The thought made me want to turn and run while there was still time.

"Tell Matt—" I hesitated. "Tell Matt I'm sorry for everything."

CHAPTER 18

I took TJ's advice and left my phone in the glove compartment of my car. Then I managed to snag a seat on a red-eye flight out of Syracuse. Eight hours later I landed in Phoenix, where I rented a car. Because of the change in time, it was still dark.

On the airplane and on the two-hour drive north to Sedona, I thought a lot about Matt. I hoped he would forgive me. If I had had my phone with me, I would have called him, but maybe it was better this way. We needed some time apart. Our relationship had moved too fast. I could explain after I returned—if he would let me. I knew I would have to return. I couldn't hide in Sedona indefinitely. If I didn't finish my classes, I would not be going to Juilliard in the spring. Everything I had worked for would be lost. As for the man in black, I still had no idea who he was or what he wanted. Well, I assumed he wanted the box. I just didn't know *why*. Maybe I would find some answers in Sedona. At the same time maybe I would find out more about my mother. If she came from there, maybe someone would remember her—even if it was twenty years ago. It was a long shot, but I yearned for answers.

As I neared Sedona, the sun rose, suffusing the highway and the sprawling desert community with pink light. Looming around Sedona were the massive red rock formations for which it was famous, even more impressive than I had imagined.

By now I was hungry and tired. As I entered the business district, I spotted a pancake house where I could get some breakfast. There were only a few other customers when I entered. I chose a small window table and ordered waffles and a cup of coffee. The coffee smelled wonderful. I couldn't wait to take that first sip. The waitress who brought my food was about my age, a slim young woman in jeans with her hair pulled back in a ponytail and a quick smile. I pulled out the photo of my mother and father standing in front of the red rocks and showed it to her.

"By any chance, do you know where this was taken?" I asked.

She took the photo and studied it. "That could be part of Cathedral Rock, but I'm not positive. Or it could be in Boynton Canyon. It's sort of a strange angle, so I'm not certain."

"Can you tell me how to find those places?"

"Sure. Hang on a sec. I'll get a map."

I was eager to find the rocks, so I decided to postpone exploring Sedona until later. I followed the souvenir map the waitress had given me. After wandering about for almost an hour on backroads, I thought I spotted the rocks in the distance. I pulled my rental car off the road onto the gravel shoulder, got out, and stared at them. They were too far away to trek to, and I didn't have the right kind of shoes for the rugged terrain, so walking to them would have to wait for another day. But just the sight of them made me feel hopeful that I would find some answers. I stood there a few more minutes, alone except for a hawk soaring overhead. Around me the trees and rocks spread out in every direction, the red rock formations thrusting up against the blue sky like the petrified handiwork of a race of giants.

After gazing my fill, I climbed back in the rental car and headed back to Sedona. Since it was much too early to check in to a hotel, I decided to explore the shops. I thought I might be able to find a box like my mother's if it had come from Sedona. I wandered in and out of small shops selling everything from turquoise and silver jewelry to psychic readings, crystals, and jeep tours. The sun was higher and hotter than it had been earlier, the sidewalks and shops more crowded with tourists, and there was more traffic on 89A, the highway that ran through town. But after an hour or more of searching, I still hadn't run across a box like my mother's.

Finally, in a large souvenir shop, after browsing among shelves crowded with mugs, T-shirts, caps, crystals, scented candles, and books about New Age spirituality, I approached a clerk who stood behind the counter. She was a striking Native American woman of middle age with a long black braid hanging down her back. At her ears dangled earrings with white feathers, and around her neck she wore a crystal pendant on a chain.

"I'm looking for a box," I said and indicated the size with my hands. "Something unusual made of a material like aluminum."

"Aluminum?" She frowned.

"Well, it's shiny but not really aluminum."

"Everything we have is here." She waved a hand toward the shelves of merchandise.

"I thought you might have . . ." I stopped. Had I really expected to walk into a shop and see a box like my mother's sitting on a shelf for sale to tourists?

"Perhaps you would like a psychic reading?" she suggested, drawing my attention to a small sign on the counter that said AURAS READ (Special Price $29).

"I don't think so . . ." I didn't want to offend her, but I had no desire to waste money on an aura reading. It was silly to think people emitted colored auras, on a par with believing in astrology and Ouija boards.

"Have you ever had your aura read before?" she asked.

"Well, no," I admitted.

"Then why not try it?" She smiled. She might have been trying to entice a picky child to eat an exotic food.

"I don't believe in it," I said bluntly.

"You don't have to. It works all the same whether you do or don't."

I shook my head. "I only wanted to find a certain box."

"Why is this box so important to you?"

I hesitated. I doubted she could help me, but what if she could? What if this was my one and only opportunity to solve the mystery of my mother's box, and I passed it up because I was skeptical of aura readings and other dubious New Age fads? What did I have to lose? I unzipped my backpack and lifted out the box. "I'm looking for a box like this."

"So you already have a box. You're not really looking for another one, are you?"

"I'm trying to find someone who can tell me about this box. I think it may have come from around here. I thought you might recognize it."

"It's sealed," she said.

"Yes."

"What's inside?"

"I don't know."

She studied it thoughtfully. "Why do you think it came from here?"

I opened my wallet, removed the photograph, and laid it on the counter between us. "That's my mother and father. See, there's the box." I pointed at the sliver of light behind them.

She studied the photo. "How can you be sure it's this box?"

"I just am." I started to zip the box back into my bag.

"I'll give you fifty for it, just the way it is."

We looked at each other. Her dark eyes gave nothing away.

"It's not for sale."

She shrugged. "Let me know if you change your mind. The same for the aura reading."

A noisy group of young people chose that moment to invade the shop. I slipped my arms into the straps of my backpack and headed for the door. When I looked back at her, she was watching me. I walked out of the shop, no nearer to the answers I sought.

* * *

I had left home with nothing but my violin, my mother's box, and the clothes on my back. No toothbrush, no deodorant, no change of underwear. I needed to find a store where I could buy these things, so I drove down 89A until I spotted a grocery store and a drugstore. Soon I had the necessities I was missing.

Now it was time to find a place to stay. Sedona had lots of hotels, motels, and resorts, but October turned out to be part of the busy tourist season, and that made it more difficult than I expected to find a room. But, after much hunting, due to a last-minute cancellation, I found one in a hotel on the outskirts of Sedona. Although it was more expensive than I had hoped for, by this time I was just grateful to have found a room.

The first thing I did after checking in was take a shower. It's amazing how much better a shower can make you feel when you are hot, dusty, and tired. Revived, I ventured out again in search of dinner. In the heart of Sedona I found a restaurant with open-air tables under an awning where I could watch people walk by as I dined on lasagna and sipped lemonade.

Afterward I didn't feel like going back to my room yet, so I drove around some more. It was starting to get dark now. I saw young people hanging out in front of a bar, smoking and laughing. The sight of them made me feel lonely. A few blocks farther I saw a young couple holding hands. The guy reminded me of Matt, and I felt a pang of regret.

With nothing else to do, I returned to my hotel. Once I was back in my room, I turned on the TV and flipped through the channels, but the programs all seemed boring, so I turned it off again and lay staring up at the ceiling, asking myself why it had seemed like such a good idea to make this journey. Coming to Sedona had been a wild goose chase. Who was I kidding? I wasn't going to find anyone who knew my parents. There weren't any answers for me here. The only thing I had succeeded in doing was eluding the man in black who had chased me to my car in the rain, and that might be only a short reprieve. If he *was* a federal agent, he would track me down sooner or later. At best Sedona was a temporary sanctuary.

To distract myself from these negative thoughts, I took my violin out of its case and ran my hand lightly along its smooth surface. Just touching it comforted me. The room wasn't soundproof, but I couldn't resist tucking my violin under my chin and drawing my bow across the strings. The note I drew forth hung in the air, quivering like a live thing, and instantly I felt my spirits lift. The sound of my violin never failed to calm and console me. Playing it was like speaking in another language, one that was pure sound. I closed my eyes and let my bow coax forth several more notes..

In response someone banged on the wall beside me, three blows—*knock knock knock*—shattering my moment of respite and bringing me down to earth with a thud. I was mortified. I hadn't meant to disturb anyone. Gently I lay my violin back in its case. In the aftermath of the knocks on the wall the silence seemed deafening. How ironic that I could fill the silence with mindless TV noise but not music. At least there was no more banging on the wall. Feeling defeated, I stretched out on the bed and soon fell into a deep exhausted sleep.

CHAPTER 19

When I woke the next day, I resolved to search for answers. I had breakfast at the same pancake house as on the previous day. The same friendly waitress waited on me. She remembered me and asked if I had found the rocks I was looking for. I told her I thought I had and thanked her again for helping me.

After breakfast I poked about in more souvenir shops, searching for boxes like mine and showing any salesclerks who looked forty or older the photograph of my parents, hoping they might recognize my mother.

I bought a sturdy pair of hiking boots at a store specializing in outdoor sports gear, and after grabbing lunch at an eatery where I could sit on a balcony and enjoy a view of red rock formations, I headed out of town to see if I could get a closer view of the rocks and find the ones in my parents' photo. I had picked up a guidebook that showed me how to get to various trails. After driving on backroads and getting lost a few times, I found a route that I thought would take me to the rocks in the photograph. I left my car at a dusty gravel trailhead, then followed the trail. But instead of taking me to the rocks, the trail led to a cave. At the entrance a young couple were taking selfies.

"Did you go in?" I asked them.

"Sure," said the young man. "We come here every year on our anniversary to renew our vows." He had a ponytail and wore a bandana wrapped across his forehead. His companion had burgundy highlights in her hair and a tattoo of a shooting star on her shoulder. Both were sunburned.

"Are you from around here?" I asked.

"Sacramento. How about you?"

"Upstate New York."

"Cool."

"What's it like in there?" I asked, nodding toward the cave.

The young man shrugged. "Tight in places. You have to watch your step. This your first time?"

"Yes."

"It's a spiritual place."

"The air sings," the girl said.

I must have looked puzzled because she added, "It's the ley lines."

I knew about ley lines—mystical lines of energy that were supposed to converge around Sedona. I mentally tagged the couple as New Agers.

"Just reach out," the girl said, stretching out her arms and turning her face up to the sky like a sun worshipper. "Don't you feel it?"

I didn't, but I smiled and nodded. It was nice to run into friendly people in a place where I didn't know anybody. They were still taking selfies when I entered the cave. It took a moment for my eyes to adjust to the dim interior. It was cooler here. The mouth was spacious, but the cave soon narrowed into a low-ceilinged passageway. Up ahead I could hear voices. I hesitated, debating whether to continue. I've never liked confined spaces. The young man from Sacramento had said it was tight in places. It already seemed tight. What if it got tighter? And darker? Suddenly exploring a cave on my own seemed risky. I turned around and hastened back to the entrance.

When I stepped out of the cave, the young couple from Sacramento who had been taking selfies a few minutes earlier were walking back to their car. I was glad they hadn't witnessed my ignominious retreat.

I took several deep breaths, relieved to be back in the sunlight with the blue sky overhead. I decided I had had enough of cave exploring.

I spent another hour or two hiking trails and looking out at the landscape, searching for rock formations that might match those in the photograph. My mind kept going back to the Native American woman who had offered to buy my mother's box. I wondered what kind of psychic readings she did. The truth was I wanted answers and I wasn't finding any. Why not try a psychic reading? What would it hurt?

When I returned to Sedona, I went back to the souvenir shop I had been in the day before. The Native American woman with the long black braid stood behind the counter again.

"Change your mind about that box?" she said when I walked up to the counter where she waited.

"No." I pulled out my credit card.

"What's that for?"

I pointed to the small sign on the counter. "How about an aura reading?"

"I thought you didn't believe in it."

"I don't, but let's say I'm curious."

She called into the back and a girl of about fourteen appeared, a younger version of herself, maybe a daughter. Leaving the girl to watch the counter, she ushered me behind a faded curtain where there was just room for two folding chairs and a small round table with a white candle on it. After lighting the candle with a match, she pulled out a small leather pouch. From the pouch she shook out five oblong crystals similar to the one she wore on a chain around her neck.

"I thought you were going to read my aura," I said, puzzled.

"So I am, but I'm going to use these too."

She spread them out on the table, then moved them about as if trying to decide how to position them. When she was satisfied, she sat for a moment quietly studying them.

"I see a journey," she said.

Inwardly I groaned. *Really?*

". . . and a stranger from a far place."

I felt disappointed. It was trite fortune-telling stuff. But what had I expected?

"And music. Do you play an instrument?"

That was a lucky guess. "Violin," I conceded. "Do you see anything about the box?"

"The box? No. Should I?"

I sighed. So much for answers. Then I remembered the couple from Sacramento I had met outside the entrance to the cave. "What can you tell me about these ley lines?"

She narrowed her eyes, studying me. The candle flame lit the sharp planes of her face, making her look like a gypsy fortuneteller. "What do you want to know about them?"

I wasn't sure what I wanted to know. Ley lines were no more real than auras or crystals with magic powers, so why was I asking?

I stood. She looked up at me.

"I haven't read your aura."

"I changed my mind."

By now it was late afternoon. I decided to drive back into the desert to watch the sun set. Once I found a likely pull-off with a scenic view and no other cars, I didn't have long to wait. I got out and leaned against the car. As the sun slipped lower, the sky caught fire and the rocks burned red. I watched until the sun dipped below the horizon. Undeniably this corner of the world had a beauty all its own. I watched as a hawk floated against the darkening sky, wings outspread, like the final stroke of an artist's brush on a landscape masterpiece.

It was almost dark when I started back. In town I bought a pizza at an Italian restaurant and took it back to my hotel room, where I ate it while watching the news on TV. Two policemen had been shot in Texas, protests were taking place in Russia, there had been a terrorist attack in Afghanistan. When it ended, I turned the TV off. I would have liked to take my violin out, but I didn't want to disturb anyone on the other side of the wall again.

For a while I read a paperback mystery I had picked up at the airport. When I grew bored with it, my thoughts turned to Matt. I regretted not having explained myself better. At the same time I could hear Mr. Hajek's voice in my head telling me that I must focus harder on my goal if I wanted to succeed as a professional violinist. It was what I wanted, wasn't it? But then why did I feel so miserable?

I didn't want to be like my mother and father, who had rushed into marriage after a mere ten days. I didn't want to end up like my mother, whose life had been cut so tragically short. Had she worried about her future as a violinist? Had she had any doubts about rushing so impulsively into marriage and motherhood? Had it occurred to her that her choice might cost her her life? And having made that choice, couldn't she have left behind something by which I could know her?

But maybe she had. My eye fell on my backpack sitting on the bed. I reached for it and unzipped it, then lifted out the box. It gleamed in the light from the lamp on the stand beside me. Nowhere in the shops of Sedona had I seen anything remotely like it. It really was unique. I ran my fingers along the smooth metallic surface. It was cool to the touch. Under my fingers I could feel the fine markings that encircled it just below the tape. What if it did hold letters or photos that belonged to my mother? What if it held the answers I was looking for? I examined the tape more closely. The only way I was ever going to know was to open it.

So why was I waiting? All the arguments for not opening it suddenly seemed flimsy. What was really stopping me?

Nothing. Only my own lack of resolve. So why not just do it? Before I could change my mind, I tried to pry the tape up with my fingernails. After a few moments of fruitless effort, I gave up and looked about for something I could use. I emptied my purse. The sharpest object I could find was a pen. For a while I struggled to wedge it under the tape. I didn't want to scratch the box, but I had wondered for so long what was in it that I was willing to risk a few scratches.

Finally I got a strip of tape pried up enough to start peeling it off with my fingernails. Inch by inch it came away. I felt more determined the more I progressed. Nothing was going to stop me now. I would tear the tape off and find out once and for all what was in the box. I should have done it before, but I had held the box in such awe. My awe was gone now. I would find out what was in it. And if it was empty? After so much speculation it would be a disappointment, but better to know than to keep wondering.

When the last bit of tape fell away, I paused, my heart beating fast. The box sat beside me on the bed, looking strangely bare with the tape removed. I half expected to find the lid still sealed, but instead it lifted off easily. There was an explosion of white light accompanied by a burst of the most beautiful music I had ever heard, like a violin, a Stradivarius maybe. No, something rarer and richer, maybe not a violin at all. It brought tears to my eyes. What a gorgeous sound! And the light show was breathtaking. As I watched in wonder, I saw that it was made up of many small moving pinpoints of light. It was unlike anything I had ever seen, and yet it seemed somehow familiar.

Then someone rapped on my door. I groaned. No doubt I had disturbed my neighbor again. Hastily I clapped the lid back on, extinguishing the light and stopping the music. I sat for a moment breathless, willing my disgruntled neighbor to go away. Instead he—or she—rapped louder.

I didn't want to deal with an angry hotel guest. Not now at any rate. I wanted to be alone to think about what I had just seen and heard. Stealing to the door, I put my eye to the peephole. The image I saw was distorted, like a reflection in a fun-house mirror. I got an impression of smooth good looks, a shock of blond hair, a white shirt. But I had no intention of opening the door. Let him bang away all he wanted.

He must have realized I wasn't going to open up because after a few minutes he left. I heaved a sigh of relief, grateful to have avoided an unpleasant confrontation.

I looked back at the box with regret. I would have to leave the lid on for now. At least I knew that the box didn't contain something dangerous like a bomb. I had no idea what it *did* contain, but anything so beautiful could not possibly be harmful. I didn't know what kind of mechanism could cause such a display of light and sound, but as soon as I figured out a place where I could open the box without attracting attention, I would open it again and take a closer look.

CHAPTER 20

My first thoughts when I woke were of the box. Where could I take it to open it? A soundproof room like my practice room back at the university would have been ideal, but where could I find a soundproof room in Sedona? No, I would have to take the box into the desert to open it. Anywhere where there were people about would be impossible. I had to keep the box away from prying eyes, to find somewhere isolated where tourists or hikers wouldn't stumble upon me. Surely in the desert I could find a place like that.

Impatient to put my plan into action, I decided to eat breakfast in the hotel dining room instead of driving to the pancake house. It would be faster, and I would be on my way sooner.

The hotel dining room was more crowded than I expected. I had my eye on one of the last empty tables as I hurried through the line and felt relieved when I managed to claim it. I had just sat down with my plate of scrambled eggs and coffee when I noticed a blond well-built young man walk in—the sort that makes heads turn in a crowded room. He scanned the room—maybe for someone he knew or maybe for a free table. I lowered my eyes, pretending to be engrossed in my scrambled eggs. Could he be the blond-haired man who banged on my door the night before? I asked myself. Even if he was, there was no reason to alarmed. I hadn't opened my door, so he hadn't seen me. He had no way of knowing I was responsible for the noise that had disturbed him.

I stole glances at him as he made his way down the buffet line. Once he had his plate full, he looked around again. But there were no more free tables. Then his eye fell on the free chair at my table and he started toward me. I felt a wave of panic. I didn't want him to choose my table. But, of course, he already had. Within seconds he was standing over me, and I couldn't ignore him any longer.

"Would you mind?" he asked politely, indicating the chair. He was even more handsome up close.

I could have said yes, I minded, but it would have been rude. He could see that I was alone. It wasn't as if I was saving the chair for someone, and I wasn't going to lie and say I was. I would have to make the best of it. So I forced myself to smile and say, "Of course not."

Most young women in my place would no doubt have welcomed having such a hot guy join her for breakfast, but I didn't want to flirt or make small talk. I just wanted to be left alone to think about the box while I ate my breakfast. But apparently that was not to be.

I sighed and resigned myself to sharing my table.

"Are you from out of state?" he asked after he was seated and had taken a gulp of his coffee.

"Yes," I answered reluctantly, then added, "Upstate New York.," because it seemed impolite not to. And since he had inquired about me, good manners dictated that I inquire about him. "And you?"

"Canada."

For a fleeting second I remembered the Native American woman at the souvenir shop predicting I would meet a stranger from far away. Coincidence, I told myself. She probably doled that out to every unmarried young woman gullible enough to request a reading. But knowing he was from another country made me more conscious of an obligation to be polite. "My mother came from Canada," I said, then bit my tongue. I didn't even know if that was true, but it was too late to take it back.

"What part of Canada?" he asked as he cut into a slice of French toast on his plate.

He had blue eyes I noticed when he looked up—intense eyes that gave me the feeling he would know if I was telling the truth or not, but he was quick to smile, so I relaxed.

"I'm not sure," I said, realizing a second later that if my mother came from Canada, I should probably be able to say from where in Canada.

I tried to deflect attention away from myself. "How about you?"

"British Columbia."

"What brings you to Sedona?"

"Business." Brief and to the point. He had lobbed the ball back into my court. I tried again.

"What sort of business?"

"Communications equipment."

"Like cell phones?"

He smiled. "Something like that. What about you?"

I thought quickly, trying to come up with an answer that would sound plausible. "Research." I could be brief too. There were advantages to brevity. Fewer details to get tripped up over.

"What kind of research?"

"Family research." Which was true, sort of. There was no reason to mention that I was hiding out from shadowy government agents, was there?

"Your family's from around here?"

"My mother."

He looked puzzled. "I thought you said she was from Canada."

Oops. Caught. Think quickly.

"She came from Canada to here. To Sedona." I took a sip of coffee, hoping he didn't ask more questions about my mother's background.

"So how do you do your research?"

This question was just as bad as ones about my mother's background. What was I supposed to say—I had shown a few random strangers a photograph of her and my father standing in front of some red rocks? *That* was my research? No wonder I hadn't turned up any useful leads.

"I've been looking for people who might have known her," I said. Did that sound as lame to him as it did to me?

"Have any luck?" He took a bite of French toast and fixed me with those disconcerting blue eyes again. He seemed genuinely interested in my response.

"Not really," I admitted.

"Oh, what am I thinking?" He hit his forehead lightly with the heel of his hand. "I haven't even introduced myself. Val Halderman." He thrust a hand across the table, and I had no choice but to put down my coffee and shake it.

"Lauren Ferguson."

"And is it your first time to visit Sedona, Lauren? That is, if you don't mind my asking."

"It is. And you?"

"My first time too. And I'm very much looking forward to checking out the sights."

"Like the red rocks?" I suggested.

"That's right. Have you seen them?"

"Of course. They're all around us."

He grinned. "Of course, they are. I meant closer up."

"Yes. They're not far from here. They practically surround Sedona."

"Great. Maybe you can give me directions. Have you been to any of the caves?"

"Yes. No. Not exactly."

He looked as if he were trying not to laugh. "Sorry. You looked so alarmed."

I sighed. "I started to go into a cave and changed my mind."

He raised an eyebrow. "Oh?"

"I don't like tight closed-in spaces."

"Who does?" He looked about the room. It was still crowded. "Look, I don't mean to be forward, but are you here by yourself? Because if you are, maybe we could go see some of the sights together. What do you say?"

His offer took me by surprise. I tried to think quickly how to refuse without sounding rude. He seemed nice enough, but I didn't know him. He could be a serial killer or mass murderer for all I knew. I was alone in a strange place, and I should be careful. Besides, I was looking forward to opening the box again. Playing tour guide to a man I had just met over breakfast—even if he looked like a Norse god—was not on my agenda.

"For the record, I'm not a serial killer. Just in case that's what you're thinking. Honest."

I felt guilty and tried to cover up. "I sort of have other plans."

"Right. Your family research."

"Well, yes."

"Tell you what. Come see the sights with me, and then I'll help you with your research. I promise."

He looked so hopeful across the table that I felt reluctant to turn him down. After all, I could always open the box later. It wasn't like it was urgent. I knew what was in it now. It was a sort of light show and music box combined—a very ingenious device, and I was dying to get a second look at it, but I doubted it would tell me anything about my mother. Why not take this opportunity to explore the area? My parents had been here—had maybe *met* here, if Aunt Nora was right. Chances were they had explored the area too. If I took Val Halderman up on his offer, I would see what they had seen, and maybe when I had, I would understand them a little better.

CHAPTER 21

Val had to run a mysterious errand before we started off, but then we were on our way. Of course, in typical male fashion he insisted on driving his own rental vehicle, a red Jeep of which he seemed quite fond. I sat in the passenger seat and told him where to turn. I could hardly believe I had agreed to go sightseeing with someone I barely knew. But it was not as if we were going to spend all day together. I could give him a few hours of my time and then in the afternoon search for a place in the desert to open the box. In the meantime I would relax and enjoy the outing. I could do that, couldn't I?

Val proved to be surprisingly easy to talk to. By the time we reached our first trailhead, I had told him about losing my grandfather, being an only child, and my plans to enroll in Juilliard in the spring.

I was glad now that I had agreed to explore the sights together. As he said, it was more interesting to explore a new place with someone else. He pointed out rock formations I hadn't noticed when I was exploring on my own. He took turnoffs that I would have passed by. He struck up conversations with people who stopped at the same pull-offs we stopped at. He was naturally gregarious, friendly to everyone he met. In fact, it was hard to imagine him ever spending his time alone. With his quick smile and good looks, he attracted people. And because he attracted people, I began to wonder if he had a wife or a girlfriend. When I got up enough nerve to ask, he laughed.

"I travel a lot," he said, which did not answer my question.

He didn't wear a ring, but then not all married men do. It was hard to believe that he was unattached. Not that it mattered. We were just hanging out together for a morning, and after we went our separate ways, we would probably never see each other again. His personal life was none of my business.

Before long we came to the trailhead that led to the cave where I had gone the day before. There were half a dozen cars and pickup trucks parked in the gravel parking area.

"Are you up for this?" Val asked, glancing at me as he turned off the engine.

"I'll wait for you here," I told him. "But you go in if you want."

"It's too hot to wait in the Jeep," he protested.

"Then I'll wait near the mouth of the cave."

"Are you sure? There's probably not much shade."

"I'll be fine. Don't worry about me."

We climbed out then and started up the trail.

When we reached the red rocks where I thought my parents had snapped their photo, he pulled out his cell phone and insisted on a selfie of us in front of the rocks. It seemed odd to be posing in the same place my mother and father may have posed for a photo. What's more, the box was behind us, just as it had been behind them in their photo, but this time concealed in my backpack. I hadn't wanted to leave it in the hotel room for fear it might get stolen. It seemed safer to keep it with me. So there it was in the selfie, although I was the only one who knew that.

After taking the selfie, we turned our attention to the nearby cave.

"How far did you go the other time?" Val asked as we neared the entrance. A couple with two children and a dog were taking photos next to a *No Vandalism* sign.

"Not far."

"Was there anything to see?"

"I don't know. It started to narrow and I got scared."

"Maybe it would be different if you had somebody with you."

I hesitated, feeling a little embarrassed. Maybe I *had* overreacted. Maybe I should try again. He was right. It might be different if I had somebody with me.

"Okay," I said, "but if I start to feel claustrophobic, I'm coming back."

"Fair enough."

The mouth of the cave was wide. Three hikers coming out passed us, barely breaking their stride. Val asked them how far back the cave went. "Maybe five hundred yards," said one. "You can feel the energy. It's awesome."

Soon the cave began to narrow. Val reached for my hand. "Just take a few deep breaths."

This was the part where I had panicked and turned back the day before. Somehow it didn't seem as bad with Val holding my hand. He exuded strength and confidence. I told myself I could do this.

His other hand held a flashlight, which he swung about, illuminating the walls. They were so close we had to walk single file.

"You okay?"

"I think so." I was inching along, wondering what would happen if we met other hikers in this narrow passage. Who would back up, us or them? Was there some protocol for how to pass others in tight spaces when you were in a cave?

"I think it widens in just a bit," Val said. "Not much farther."

He proved to be right. I felt a wave of relief as the walls fell back. Suddenly I could breathe again.

"Hear that?" he said.

I listened. Somewhere ahead of us several hikers were whooping, their voices echoing as if they came from a well.

"An echo chamber," Val said, then quickly added, "Watch your step."

The floor dropped away. I nearly lost my balance, saved only by his strong arm. Suddenly I was against his chest and aware of how fast my heart was beating. He had dropped his flashlight in catching me, and it rolled across the floor, its beam careening off the walls.

"Sorry," he said as he let go and retrieved his flashlight.

We continued on, my hand in his, and I was grateful to have someone to hold onto in case there were more drop-offs ahead. I wasn't eager to sprain an ankle.

Soon we came to a cavern where the ceiling was high. Evidently this was the echo chamber we had heard a few minutes earlier.

"I think this is where the vortex is," Val said.

"Do you believe that stuff?" I asked, surprised.

He shrugged. "You have to admit there's a kind of charged feeling in the air."

If there was, I didn't feel it.

A few steps farther we were plunged into darkness so thick I couldn't see anything. I gasped. "What happened?"

"I turned off the flashlight."

"Why?"

"Just give it a minute. It's easier to feel it in the dark."

"Feel what?"

I was still holding on to his hand. In fact, you would have had trouble prying me loose. I was intensely aware of him standing there beside me in the dark and afraid to take a step for fear the ground might drop away.

Then he kissed me, and I forgot we were standing in total darkness. I couldn't have told you if I felt the energy field of a vortex. The kiss knocked everything else out of my head. I wasn't sure how I felt about kissing Val. I hadn't seen it coming, and now that it had, my thoughts were all confused.

Before I could catch my breath and collect myself, we were interrupted by two hikers coming from deeper in the cave. They were talking while the light from their flashlights bobbed along, aimed now at their feet and now at the walls. Val flipped his flashlight back on so they would see us. They hesitated a second or two and then kept coming.

"What's up ahead?" he asked as they drew abreast.

"A view," one said.

"A portal to another world," said the other, and they grinned at each other, as if sharing a private joke.

"Do we go on?" Val asked me as they tromped away.

"Why not?" I said, trying to sound more confident than I felt. "We've come this far."

He held my hand, and we followed the path by the light of his flashlight. Neither of us said anything about the kiss. I was uncertain what to think. Had he meant to kiss me or was the kiss just a spur-of-the-moment impulse? I wanted to ask, but now I felt tongue-tied and self-conscious. *Of course, he didn't mean to kiss you*, I told myself. *He's probably got a girlfriend back in Canada. And certainly you didn't mean to kiss him. Did you?*

It was that last question that bothered me most. I was still mulling it over when we rounded the next bend and emerged into sunlight so sudden and bright it made me blink. It poured in through a large gap in the wall. Through the gap we could see blue sky, rugged sandstone cliffs, a sheer drop into a canyon, and a hawk gliding across the ether.

"Look, you can see for miles," Val said.

It was a breathtaking view. I felt as if I could stand there forever, transported to an unspoiled world. Time seemed to stop.

"Aren't you glad now that you came?" he asked, his lips nearly touching my ear.

It *was* beautiful, but I had very mixed feelings at this point. If I had known Val was going to kiss me in the cave, would I have gone in with him? I had not come to Sedona looking for romance. I was already in a muddle about my feelings for Matt, and breaking up with him had been like ripping out my heart. If it had been Matt there beside me, I was not at all sure I wouldn't change my mind about breaking up with him. Val was not Matt, but still . . . *I know*—his daunting Norse god good looks should have made no difference, but I was only human.

When we finally emerged from the cave, I breathed a sigh of relief. I was determined not to let a spontaneous kiss that ought not to have happened mean more than it did. I glanced at my watch and suggested we head back to Sedona for lunch.

Val grinned. "I brought lunch along. I thought maybe we could find someplace to eat it."

He had brought lunch? Why hadn't he mentioned this earlier? I had assumed we would return to Sedona when lunchtime rolled around. I had counted on it.

"Do you have anything pressing you need to get back for?" he asked with a sideways glance.

What could I say? I was dying to open a mysterious box that had belonged to my mother? I could think of no excuse to justify rushing back to Sedona, and my failure to quickly come up with one was an admission that I had no pressing need to return.

"What about you?" I asked, remembering that he was there on a business trip. Surely he had business to attend to. A meeting? An appointment?

"I just happen to be free today," he said cheerfully, demolishing that suggestion. "But I'll take you back if you'd like. Just say the word."

I hated to be a spoilsport. And I had to admit a picnic lunch sounded tempting. I suddenly realized I was hungry. What would it hurt to have a picnic lunch, especially since he had gone to the trouble of bringing one along? Maybe I had overblown the kiss in my mind. Maybe it had meant nothing to him. Maybe he had been missing his girlfriend back home. Or his wife. I still didn't know if he was married.

So I agreed to the picnic lunch. After all, it would extend our outing by only a half hour or so, and then we would head back.

With the doors of the Jeep flung open, we ate at a nearby roadside pull-off with a spectacular view of red rock formations. Val had certainly come prepared. I was impressed. He had packed a cooler with cold turkey sandwiches and slices of Swiss cheese from a grocery store deli, grapes, carrot sticks, potato chips, a bottle of wine, and plastic cups to drink it in. He even had a blanket to spread out on the back seat for us to eat on. He had thought of everything.

"You didn't feel the energy, seriously?" he said as we devoured our movable feast.

"Seriously you did?" I retorted.

He sighed and shook his head in mock despair.

"Look, I don't want you to get the wrong idea," I said.

"The wrong idea?"

"About me."

"And what would that be?"

"I just broke up with someone. I'm not looking to get involved." There. I had been upfront and honest.

He chewed thoughtfully, looking out at the massive red rocks that jutted up in the distance. "You just broke up with a boyfriend?"

"Yes."

"I take it this was back in New York?"

"Yes."

"So what happened?"

I hesitated. It seemed disloyal to Matt to reveal the details of our breakup. "We weren't right for each other."

"So is that the real reason you're here?"

"No, I told you. My mother came from here."

He nodded. "Family research. Your Canadian mother."

I realized how unconvincing it sounded. But if I told him why I really left New York, I would have to include the man in black. And I had no intention of doing that.

"It's complicated."

"It always is."

For a few minutes we ate in silence. I wondered if he was thinking of someone *he* had broken up with.

"So tell me about this boyfriend. What's he like?"

I hesitated again. How to describe Matt? "He's very sweet. He makes me laugh."

"So why did you break up with him?"

"We were too different."

"So you said."

"I'm going to Juilliard in the spring. It wouldn't work out."

"And so you felt a sudden need to fly to Arizona to find out more about your mother. Makes perfect sense."

"I guess I needed to get away," I admitted. "I needed time to think. But the part about wanting to find out more about my mother is true. I know so little about her. I thought I might find answers here."

"But so far you haven't?"

"No."

"More wine?" He held up the bottle.

I shook my head. Better to keep a clear head.

He poured a little more in his own plastic cup. "You know what I think?"

"What?"

"I think we should have dinner tonight. You don't have other plans, do you? I saw this nice little restaurant that I'd like to check out."

"No, really. I don't think . . ."

He shrugged.

I bit my lip. "I don't know anything about you."

"What do you want to know?"

I took a deep breath. "Are you married?"

He started laughing. "That's the second time you asked me."

"Well, you didn't exactly deny it the first time."

"No, I don't have a wife," he said. "And no, I have no girlfriend waiting for me either."

"We're so different."

"Maybe not so different as you think." He reached his hand across the blanket, palm up. "Give me a chance."

Matt had said those same words.

CHAPTER 22

It was midafternoon when we got back to Sedona. I had a few hours free before dinner and used them to run out and buy a sundress and sandals to wear when we went out later. When I got back, I took the box out of my backpack and just held it on my lap for a few minutes. I wished I could open it. I wanted to see that explosion of light again and hear that amazing music, but the thought that someone beyond the wall would object stopped me. Maybe it wasn't Val on the other side of the wall. I realized now that he hadn't arrived until yesterday, and so he couldn't have pounded on the wall the evening before. And I was no longer sure he was the man I had glimpsed through the peephole. But whoever was on the other side of the wall, I didn't want to draw their attention again. Later I could drive into the desert, open the box, and watch and listen to my heart's content. I just had to be patient a little longer.

The restaurant Val took me to was not much to look at on the outside but surprisingly cozy on the inside with leather booths, Tiffany-style hanging lamps, and a singer in a cowboy hat perched on a stool strumming a guitar.

Val too had changed clothes and looked suavely handsome. He wore a white shirt—no tie—his hair still damp from a shower. I thought I caught a whiff of cologne as I slid into the booth across from him with my backpack.

"You seem very attached to that," he observed.

"It goes where I go. I don't want to lose it."

"What's inside must be very important."

"It is. To me."

"Now you've made me curious."

"It's an old family heirloom."

He raised an eyebrow but I didn't elaborate.

I glanced around the room. The Tiffany lamps gave it a nice ambiance. The room was dimly lit with pools of muted light. I liked the laid-back style of the cowboy singer, who was crooning a song about heartbreak and second chances.

"This is nice, isn't it?" Val said after we had placed our order.

"How did you find it?" I asked.

"The girl at the hotel desk recommended it."

"Good choice."

"And I'm hoping I can talk you into a chamber music concert afterward. There's one tonight at the Arts Center. Mozart. A string quartet. I just happen to have tickets." He pulled them from his pocket and flashed them as proof.

"Just happen to?"

"I'd hate for them to go to waste."

"Mozart?"

"Yes."

"You like classical music?"

"Of course. Don't you?"

This was an aspect of Val that I would never have suspected. Aside from fellow music students, I had never met a guy before who claimed to like classical music, certainly not one who looked like Val. Was he telling the truth or trying to impress me? But why try to impress me? He could have gotten just about any girl he set his sights on.

"How long will you be here?" he asked.

"I haven't decided. Maybe a few days."

"And then what?"

"I go back."

"To your boyfriend?"

I shook my head. "That's over. We broke up. But I have to finish the term."

"What would happen if you didn't finish the term?"

I think my heart stopped. What was he suggesting? I had to go back. I had to finish my coursework if I wanted to go to Juilliard in the spring. Even if it meant facing down the man in black, I had to go back.

Val reached across the table and touched my bare arm. I shivered. Our eyes met and locked. I had the impression he was about to say something important, but I have no idea what because at that moment a waitress brought our food. That gave me a chance to take a few deep breaths. *Steady*, I told myself. *We just met.*

"I know you think this is moving too fast," he said when we were alone again. "But I don't have very long."

We had known each other for less than twenty-four hours.

"People don't just meet and fall in love and throw everything they've ever worked for overboard," I said.

"Some people do." He looked at me evenly.

I thought of my parents. Was this what it had been like for them? I tried to calm my racing thoughts. What did I know of Val? What did he know of me? Yes, it was all happening too fast. We needed to slow down.

"You don't know anything about me," I said, dipping my spoon into a bowl of French onion soup. I hoped my hand wasn't shaking.

"I know you just broke up with your boyfriend. And that your grandfather died recently. And that you're seeking answers about your mother." The light from the Tiffany lamp over the table fell on his face. His blue eyes watched me intently. "I know you're very talented . . ."

"You don't know that," I objected.

"But I do. You have never felt you belonged. You live for your violin. You're only really happy when you're playing it."

I tried to remember if I had told him these things about myself, or did he guess all this about me? Could he see through me so clearly?

"You haven't told me much about yourself," I said. "All I know is that you're from Canada and you sell smartphones."

"Not exactly smartphones."

"Communication devices."

"And I like classical music."

"And you like classical music."

He smiled. "So you'll go with me to the chamber music concert?"

* * *

The box would just have to wait a little longer. There would be time later to drive into the desert and open it. Meanwhile, the concert was a wonderful treat, and I was glad Val had invited me. Mozart had always been one of my favorite composers. His music was so joyous and playful. As we sat on folding chairs in the small auditorium listening to the string quartet, I kept glancing at Val, who seemed to be enjoying the music just as much as I was. I was pretty sure he wasn't faking it. The hour and a half flew by, and then it was over.

"I wish I could hear *you* play," Val said as we walked back to his rented Jeep.

"Haven't you had enough music for tonight?" I said.

"I don't suppose you brought your violin with you when you ran away?"

"Actually I did, but it's late and I'm sure the other hotel guests wouldn't appreciate a nighttime serenade." I thought of the person who had banged on the wall the night I had played a few notes on my violin and the man I had glimpsed through the peephole the night I opened the box.

"I've got an idea," Val said. "We could go into the desert and you could play your violin under the stars and we wouldn't bother anybody."

I was ready to say no, but then it struck me that going into the desert to hear music was precisely what I had wanted to do ever since opening the box. True, I would have to wait a little longer to open the box again if I went with Val, but the idea of playing my violin under the stars stirred me in a way I would find hard to explain. How could I resist a suggestion like that?

CHAPTER 23

After a quick trip back to the hotel to retrieve my violin, we set off to find a secluded spot in the desert. As we sped along the highway in the dark, I thought how strange it was to be heading into the desert with Val to play my violin. It was hard to believe I had only met him that morning. I felt as if my future were rushing toward me, and I wasn't sure I was ready for it.

We had been on the road for about five minutes when Val glanced over at me and broke the silence. "What are you thinking so hard about?"

"How unpredictable life is."

"And how is it unpredictable?"

"Well, if I hadn't suddenly decided to fly to Sedona when I did, and if you hadn't flown here on a business trip, we might never have met."

"Maybe we were fated to meet." He grinned. "Did that occur to you?"

"I don't believe in fate."

He glanced at me again. "Have you ever felt you are living in a world where you don't belong?"

"What do you mean?"

"I mean, do you ever feel you belong somewhere else?"

This question made me uncomfortable. "Doesn't everybody sometimes?"

He was silent a minute. "Have you ever asked yourself why you're so drawn to the violin?"

"That's easy. My mother played the violin."

"Did she?"

"They say she was very good at it."

"I'll bet she was. Would you ever give it up?"

"My violin? I couldn't."

"But suppose someone asked you to—someone you cared about very much."

"I couldn't."

"Suppose you could live in a place where everyone understood how you felt about your violin because that's how they felt about it too?"

"I can't imagine a place like that."

"What if I told you there *is* a place like that?"

"You mean Canada?" I rolled my eyes, but he didn't laugh.

He fell silent again, his eyes fixed on the narrow winding road before us with its hairpin turns and precipitous drop-offs.

Suddenly I felt uneasy. Surely he didn't expect me to drop everything and run off to Canada with him? I liked him, but I hardly knew him. People didn't just drop everything and run off with a total stranger.

Then he smiled and I relaxed. I had taken him too seriously. He was teasing me, not suggesting I run off to

Canada with him. Before us the rocks loomed up against the night sky like alien monoliths. He turned off the road at a scenic pull-off and stopped the Jeep. I climbed out and retrieved my violin case from the back seat.

"Look at that," Val said, tipping his head back and looking up at the stars. The Milky Way lay in a broad swath across the sky. It was a perfect night for star-gazing, not a cloud in the sky.

"There's Pisces," he said, pointing.

"And Pegasus," I added.

He grinned. "You're full of surprises."

"And so are you."

A smile played at the corner of his lips. "I told you. We're more alike than you think."

I took my violin and bow from the case and tucked my violin under my chin. I closed my eyes and let my fingers find the notes and my bow draw them forth. It was amazing to hear Beethoven's Violin Sonata in the open air under the stars. The music seemed to expand in all directions and carry me with it. My violin had never sounded so clear in a soundproof practice room or a concert hall. I felt like I was a part of the universe, part of the flow of some great current of life and being. Then I opened my eyes and looked up at the sky and saw the millions of stars spread out above me. In that instant I remembered the explosion of light from my mother's box and the strange and beautiful music that accompanied it. I knew in a flash what I had seen. A map of the stars. I didn't know how it was possible, but I was as certain of it as I was of anything in the world. But I didn't stop playing my violin. I kept going, pouring out the rest of the sonata until I reached the last note.

Val was smiling when I finished. For a minute neither of us spoke.

"You don't belong here," he said quietly. "Surely you know that."

"Where do I belong?"

"With your own kind."

"What's that supposed to mean?"

Instead of answering, he pulled me close. Then he kissed me, a long kiss that made me feel like I was floating out of myself. I stood there, awkwardly clutching my violin in one hand, my bow in the other, my arm flung around his neck. At that moment throwing everything over for him didn't seem so crazy. He understood me in a way no one else ever had. Matt had tried to understand, but the passion I felt for music was incomprehensible to him. Val understood. I didn't know how or why, but he did. Maybe he harbored some secret he wasn't telling me. Maybe he played an instrument. That was the only explanation I could think of for how he could understand so perfectly what music meant to me.

"Come back with me," he murmured against my hair.

I had been fighting my feelings for him all day, reluctant to let myself fall in love again, fearful that it would be just as futile as falling in love with Matt had been. But what if it wasn't? What if it was the right choice this time? Suppose I didn't go back—not even for Juilliard. Suppose I chose Canada and Val. The enormity of such a decision rose up before me as solidly as one of those red rocks jutting up against the night sky.

His lips moved up my jaw to my ear. "You are so much like your mother," he said softly into my hair.

For a second I thought I had heard wrong. Mr. Merrick had said I was so much like my mother. But he had *known* my mother. Val had never known her. Or had he?

I pulled back and stared at him. He stood there with a rueful smile while I hugged my violin to my chest, my thoughts churning. A doubt crept into my mind. Maybe meeting him had not been a coincidence. What had he said? Maybe we were fated to meet? He was supposedly in Sedona to sell communication devices, but he had had the whole day free. Was that too a coincidence?

"Why are you here?" I asked. "And don't tell me it's because of the vortexes."

"You don't know? I'm here because of you."

"What do you mean?" I felt my skin crawl.

"You opened a door, and I came through."

"What door? What are you talking about?" I tried to tamp down my panic.

But I knew. He meant my mother's box. I remembered the banging on my door when I lifted the lid. It was Val I saw through the peephole. I was certain now. Val had been banging on my door last night.

"You're not from Canada."

"No."

"So where are you from?"

He pointed at the sky, at the Milky Way. What had the Native American woman said? *I see a journey and a stranger from a far place.* A shiver ran down my spine.

"You don't belong here," he said again. "I've come to take you home."

I shook my head. "No, I am home."

At that moment the precariousness of my situation dawned on me. I was on a sparsely traveled road miles from the outskirts of Sedona. If he refused to drive me back, how would I get back to the hotel? Could I walk it in the dark in my sandals? Doubtful. Would there be a passing car I could flag down to get a ride? I had seen no other cars since we stopped.

"Will you take me back to the hotel now?" I asked, trying to keep my voice steady.

"If that's what you want."

"It is."

I climbed back in the Jeep and sat as pressed against the passenger door as my seatbelt would allow, my violin case clutched to my chest.

"I think you're making a mistake," he said as he turned the key in the ignition. The engine leaped to life.

I stared stonily out the window as the dark rugged landscape rolled past. This was the only world I knew. No matter how wonderful he thought his world was, it wasn't *my* world. This one was.

"It's a map of the stars, isn't it?" I said.

"Yes, and a door . . . a portal."

"And if I open it, you appear?"

"Or someone else."

"It's a communication device."

He didn't answer. After a few minutes he said, "Look, if you're sure you won't go back, you should give the box to me. It's important for it not to fall into the wrong hands."

I thought of the man in black. Did he know what the box was? That would explain why he wanted it so badly. "It works both ways, doesn't it?"

Val let out a large sigh that was all the answer I needed.

So he wanted the box too. Maybe I should just give it to him. It was in my backpack in the back seat. He probably knew that. In fact, if he really wanted the box, he could probably just take it. There wasn't much I could do to keep it from him.

We didn't talk much during the rest of the drive back to the hotel. I suppose we were both caught up in our thoughts. I was pretty sure Val had not traveled light years for me. He had come for the box. Now he was facing the prospect of having to return without it.

He walked me to the door of my room but didn't try to come in. "If you change your mind . . ."

I nodded. I knew how to get in touch with him—open the box.

Once I was safely in my room alone with the door locked, I took the box out of my backpack and looked at it. I would not be able to open it again. I would not be able to see the star map again or listen to the otherworldly music that accompanied it. For that I was sorry. But I knew something now that I didn't know before. I knew my mother's secret. She had come here through a portal from another world. I didn't know why she had come here. Had she been running away? Was there something about our world that had attracted her? All I knew was after she came here she met my father and fell in love. Then she sealed the box so that it wouldn't open a portal and betray her whereabouts. Maybe she had intended to disable or destroy it later but had died before she could do that, or tell anyone else to.

CHAPTER 24

In the morning I knew what I had to do. The night before I had planned to skip breakfast in the hotel restaurant to avoid encountering Val. But now I headed for it at the same time as the day before. Val was already there, sitting at a table against the wall. He looked surprised to see me and even more surprised when I joined him with my tray of food.

"Did you change your mind?" he asked.

"No, but I have some questions."

"All right." He looked wary.

"What's it like there?"

His face relaxed. "You'd love it. We have a much higher level of technology and culture. We live in harmony. No wars, no poverty."

"How far away is it?"

"Fourteen light years, more or less."

"Why did my mother want to leave?"

"She was young. She wanted to know what else was out there."

"Did you know her?"

"Yes."

He looked closer to my age than to my mother's. My mother would be in her forties if she had lived. Did people age more slowly there? Had they learned how to overcome the aging of the body? Did time pass more slowly? Or was it some difference of time connected to the portal? Once I would have been eager to ask these questions, but this morning I was determined not to get distracted from what I really wanted to know.

"Were you in love with her?"

He shifted in his chair. "I was."

"Did you try to persuade her to go back?"

"I couldn't find her."

"You mean she didn't open the box."

His silence told me I had guessed right.

"Did you kill Mr. Malinsky?"

"*What?*" His eyes widened.

"Did you kill Mr. Malinsky?" I repeated.

"Who is he?"

"He was a friend of my grandfather's. A kind sweet elderly man who would never hurt anyone. Someone murdered him. He had a key to the safe deposit box where my mother's box was stored."

"Why didn't you tell me this before?" His eyes darted around the crowded room, as if a killer might be lurking nearby. "You may be in danger. All the more reason to come back with me."

"You forget. I'm my father's daughter too."

He looked as if he might argue, then shrugged. "I can't stay much longer."

"Neither can I."

I had reached this decision during the night as I wrestled with my alternatives during restless bouts of wakefulness.

"What will you do?" he asked.

"Go back."

After breakfast I drove to a hardware store and bought a roll of sealing tape. When I returned to the hotel, I carefully resealed the box. That done, it was time to go home.

I was on my way to the front desk to check out when I saw him. He was signing in. The black suit, white shirt, and tie caught my eye, and I ducked back into the elevator before he saw me. I only had a glimpse, but I would have known him anywhere. He was the man who had pursued me in the rain from the library to my car. He had tracked me down, just as I had feared he would.

I was intending to take the box back to New York with me and lock it away again in a safe deposit box, but now I realized I would have to get rid of it before he caught up with me. Unlike Val, he wouldn't allow me to choose what I wanted to do with the box. He and whatever organization he worked for had shown they were willing to kill to get their hands on it. I must not underestimate them.

To avoid running into him in the lobby, I slipped out a side door with my violin case and my backpack and headed for my rental car. Not until I had pulled out onto the street did I breathe a sigh of relief. But I still had one more thing I had to do before leaving Sedona.

I parked my car in one of the small parking lots in the tourist district and walked to the souvenir shop I had visited on my first day in Sedona. It was still early, but the shop was open. The Native American woman with the long black braid stood behind the counter, just as before. She watched without expression as I approached her.

I set my backpack on the counter, unzipped it, and removed the box. It caught the morning light streaming in from the window. "You said you would give me fifty dollars for it. Are you still interested?"

She examined the box. "The tape is different. Did you open it?"

"Yes."

"So you know what's in it?"

"Yes. Do you still want the box?"

Her eyes narrowed. I thought she would ask me what was in it, but she didn't. "Is there anything I should know about it?"

"You should be careful who you sell it to."

"Why?"

"It shouldn't fall into the wrong hands."

She was silent a moment. "I see. Anything else?"

I hesitated. "You might not want to open it."

She regarded me steadily. For a minute I thought she might refuse to take the box. But then without another word she opened her cash register, removed two twenties and a ten, and laid them on the counter. "Do you want me to read your aura now?"

"No, I don't have time," I said, picking up the bills. "But thank you for taking care of the box."

* * *

I had a lot of time to think on the long drive back to Phoenix, and more as I sat in the terminal at Sky Harbor waiting to catch a flight. I knew I was going back to the same problems I had run away from. I had no right to think Matt would forgive me. If I were him, I wouldn't forgive me. And it wouldn't take long for the man in black to figure out where I was. I just hoped it was the box he wanted and not me. I shivered to think what he and his fellow agents might do to me if they knew I carried alien DNA. I'd probably be dissected. But I was not going to give up my dream of studying at Juilliard if I could help it. I had made my choice. Here was where I wanted to be. It was the same choice my mother had made. I almost felt as if she were standing beside me cheering me on. No matter how wonderful Val's world was, *this* was the world I wanted.

It was late afternoon when the plane set down in Syracuse. Hard to believe I had been gone only four days. It seemed like so much longer. My car was parked where I had left it in the airport parking garage. My laptop and umbrella were lying on the floor in front of the passenger seat. My cell phone was stashed in the glove compartment. I tried to turn on my phone, just in case it had miraculously come back to life, but it hadn't. So even if I had text messages from Matt—which I doubted— I couldn't get to them. But getting my phone repaired would have to wait. After the long flight I just wanted to go home and sleep, and I still had at least an hour's drive ahead of me before I could do that. I needed a good night's sleep. Tomorrow would be Monday, and I didn't dare miss more classes.

The closer I got to home, the more I began to worry about what I would find. Had federal agents broken into my apartment while I was gone? Would it be a shambles again? I braced myself for the worst. But the street looked peaceful when I pulled up at the curb across from my apartment house in the gathering dusk. A teenaged boy rolled past on his skateboard, earbuds in, tuned in to music only he could hear. There was no sign of the white SUV. When I fitted my key in the lock, I heard the click of the lock releasing and felt relieved. Inside all was as it should be. The boxes of my father's things still sat neatly lined up against the wall. I moved cautiously from room to room, my confidence growing. If anyone had searched my rooms, they had left no trace.

But I was taking no chances. I barricaded the door with a chair, just as I had that night after my grandfather's funeral when my apartment had been broken into. Then after a shower and a light dinner, I again made a bed for myself on the sofa so that I would not be caught off-guard if anyone tried to break in, and I placed some kitchen knives close at hand, just in case I needed to defend myself.

CHAPTER 25

The next day I still felt jet-lagged. It was not a problem in my other classes, but it was during my violin lesson with Mr. Hajek. I knew I was unlikely to measure up to his expectations in my current condition. To make matters worse, he was in a bad mood, irritated that I had missed my lesson on Friday. I didn't tell him I had flown halfway across the country and back. I would have had to explain why, and he would not understand about the man in black or my breakup with Matt. Nor did I want to lie and claim I'd been sick. I had no good excuse to offer for missing my lesson. All I could do was apologize.

"You are not taking your lessons seriously," he scolded. "You need to decide what is important. If you are not serious, you are wasting my time and yours."

I waited, knowing the tirade would pass. It did. He sighed and ran a hand over his greying hair.

"Okay. Play the Beethoven. Let's hear it."

I expected him to interrupt me, as he often did, but he let me get all the way through the sonata without interruption.

"That's better," he said when I was finished. "It was an improvement since last time—a *slight* improvement—but an improvement all the same."

I could hardly believe my ears. Coming from him it was high praise.

After class I dropped my phone off at the service center to be repaired. On my way home I stopped by the mall to see if TJ was working. He was, although he was busy with a customer when I walked in and didn't notice me right away. When he did see me, he didn't exactly look pleased. I stayed anyway, and eventually he wandered over to where I was looking at some of the new phones.

"What are you doing here?" he asked, frowning.

"How's Matt?"

"What do you care?"

"Just tell me if he's all right."

"Yeah, he's all right. Picking up the pieces and all that."

"Did you tell him—?"

"That you were sorry? Yeah, I told him. And just for the record, next time you want to give him a message, do it yourself."

I understood why he was angry. I had handled the breakup badly. I had hurt Matt, and Matt was his friend.

After striking out with TJ, I headed for Starbucks to see if Joy was on duty. I knew she might be just as upset with me as TJ, but I didn't know who else to turn to for information about Matt. She was there behind the bar, a head taller than the other barista, looking like a fierce Amazonian warrior transported to the twenty-first century. I stood in line and ordered a latte.

"So when did you get back?" she asked as she rang me up.

"Yesterday."

"I hear you and Matt broke up."

"We did. Have you seen him?"

"Yeah. If you want to know how he's doing, you could go ask him. He's sitting over there." Her eyes slid to the right.

I was holding up the line. I stepped away with my latte and glanced in the direction she indicated. It's a wonder I hadn't noticed him when I walked in, but that was probably because his back was to me. And he wasn't alone. A girl sat across from him. A pretty girl with long black hair who was talking animatedly. He was picking up the pieces all right.

I figured it was better to leave before he saw me. As I retreated, I wondered if the girl was Sherry or someone new he had met. I was surprised he had moved on so quickly, but what had I expected? Did I think he would just wait for me to come to my senses?

Anyway, it was probably for the best. The girl with the long black hair would be everything that I wasn't. Normal and fully human for starters. And she wouldn't be inconveniently transferring to Juilliard in the spring. I had made my choice, and now I was stuck with it. I had no one to blame but myself.

I felt thoroughly miserable when I got home, but there was no time to wallow in self-pity. I had to finish that paper on Prokofiev if I wanted to ace my music history class. And if I didn't ace it, it might jeopardize my plans for Juilliard. Whether I was in the mood to finish the paper or not, I had to do it, even if it meant pulling an all-nighter, which it did. Maybe just as well. Even with the jet lag, I wasn't sure I could sleep after having seen Matt with another girl, but at least working on the paper would take my mind off him. Or so I hoped.

I muddled through classes the next day in a daze, but at least the paper was done on time. All I could think about was going back to my apartment and crashing, but as tired as I was, I still put in my practice session. After all, I had missed several days of practice when I was in Arizona. I couldn't keep letting my practice time slide. Years of violin lessons had ingrained in me the necessity to practice.

At last it was time to go home.

He must have been watching my apartment because I had hardly been in my apartment for five minutes when there was a knock on my door. My first thought was that it might be Matt, and I dashed to the door, hoping to see him standing there. But when I threw it open, I found myself face-to-face with a young man in a dark suit and tie. Not the man in black but a junior version of him. My heart sank. I was not in the mood for a chat with the feds.

"Hi," he said, smiling, and flashed a badge. "FBI. Mind if I ask you a few questions?"

I had known they would catch up with me. It was just a matter of time. He could smile and act harmless, but it didn't change the fact that one of his fellow agents may have killed Mr. Malinsky. Why had I opened my door?

"May I come in?"

I couldn't refuse. I assumed he could get a search warrant—if he didn't already have one. He could come back with his goons and break down my door if he wanted. It would only make me look guilty if I refused to allow him in.

I had to move my bedding off the sofa for him to sit down. He looked curious about the bedding but didn't ask. He glanced around the apartment. Was he looking for the box? If he was, he wouldn't find it. At least I had had the foresight to get rid of it.

"Do you mind?" he asked, pulling out his cell phone. "I'd like to record this."

I shrugged. What did it matter?

"I understand you knew Joseph Malinsky?" he began when he had set the phone to record.

"Yes."

"How well did you know him?"

"He was my grandfather's friend. Sometimes they played checkers together."

"And your grandfather died recently?"

"About a month ago."

"Sorry for your loss." He looked away, obviously uncomfortable. I wondered how new he was at this. "Do you know anyone who might have wanted to harm Joseph Malinsky?"

"The police already asked me these questions."

"I'm aware of that. But we like to be thorough. Maybe you've thought of something since then."

"No, sorry. I don't know who would kill a harmless old man like Mr. Malinsky. He wouldn't hurt a fly. They must be monsters." I looked at him pointedly.

He sighed. "Do you remember the last time you saw him?"

"At my grandfather's funeral."

"And when was that?"

"Three weeks ago."

"Did he seem uneasy? Was anything bothering him?"

"No."

"Did he say anything?"

In my mind I saw Mr. Malinsky standing in front of me that day. I felt the key he pressed into my hand. I heard his words again. *He told me if anything should happen to him, to give this to you . . . He said to be sure I gave this to you myself.*

The young FBI agent across from me was waiting expectantly. But I was not about to tell him about the key. Or the box.

"He said he was sorry about my grandfather's death."

The young agent nodded. "Sorry to have to ask you these questions. It's my job." He seemed genuinely apologetic. He turned off his phone, then stood to leave.

"Is that all?" I was surprised. Wasn't he going to ask me about the box?

He handed me a card. "If you think of anything else, call me."

I stared at it. Could it be some other FBI agents who killed Mr. Malinsky? Rogue agents he didn't know about? Should I tell him about the man in black?

While I struggled to think this through, he held out his hand. We shook hands, and then he was gone. I moved to the window and watched him walk to his car—an inconspicuous black compact. Suppose I had told him about the man in black and then found out it was just a ruse to see how much I knew? I didn't know who I could trust. He may have looked harmless, but maybe that was just to trick me.

I sighed and turned away from the window. So if the feds had not killed Mr. Malinsky, who had? I couldn't ask the police, and I couldn't ask Matt. Who did that leave? I thought of Kevin Burke. Like me, he was trying to put the pieces together. Maybe I shouldn't be so quick to dismiss him. He had been right about aliens. Maybe he had also figured out who killed Mr. Malinsky.

CHAPTER 26

I went to the Campus Corner for lunch the next day, hoping Kevin would be there, but he wasn't. Since I didn't have days to wait for him to show up, I tried to think of some way to contact him. It occurred to me that Barb Peterson might have his number. However, before I could call her, I had to get my phone back. So after violin practice, I drove to the service center to pick up my phone. The service rep, a skinny young man with hair that kept falling in his eyes, assured me it was now like new.

"What was wrong with it?" I asked.

"Oh, you got hacked," he said. "I thought you knew that."

Hacked? I had assumed it was a malfunction.

"Is there a way to tell who hacked it?" If it had been hacked, I immediately suspected the man in black or his fellow agents of being the ones responsible.

"Sorry. We just fix it. You want to sign up for our warranty plan?"

I didn't. I looked at my phone warily as I walked to my car. Could I trust it? The idea that someone might be listening in or reading my texts or email made me uneasy. I just hoped the service center had fixed the problem.

As soon as I was back in my car, I tried to phone Barb. After a few rings the call went to voicemail. I debated whether to leave a voice message or text her, then decided to just drive to her apartment building.

When I arrived, I tried to phone her again, but she still wasn't picking up. Nor did she answer the lobby buzzer for the elevator. Maybe she wasn't home, but at this point I was reluctant to give up, so I waited in the lobby until a young woman in yoga pants allowed me to ride up with her. When I got off on the fifth floor, I noticed the yellow crime scene tape still stretched across the door next to Barb's apartment. I wondered when the police would take it down.

I rang Barb's bell three times before she answered.

"Oh, it's you," she said and took off the chain lock. "I thought you might be one of those reporters. I've already told them everything I know. I just want my life to go back to normal. So do my kids." She looked down at the black cat by her foot, and the cat meowed. That was Lucifer. I assumed he was one of her *kids*.

She motioned for me to come in and cleared a chair for me to sit on. "Sorry. I wasn't expecting company." She was wearing a white terry bathrobe and fuzzy white slippers.

"I tried to call," I told her.

"Oh, I stopped answering, honey. Too many cranks. You would not believe—"

I reached down to pet Lucifer. A fluffy white cat approached more warily.

"That's Snowball. She's a sweetheart. Aren't you, baby?"

The calico was perched on a windowsill, an orange cat watched us from the kitchen doorway, and a grey tabby was curled up on top of a bookcase. I half expected to see the Cheshire cat grinning back at me from somewhere in the room.

"I thought you might know how I could get in touch with Kevin Burke," I said, getting straight to the point.

Barb brightened and visibly relaxed. "Such a sweet boy. And so considerate. He's called several times just to check on me."

"Do you have his phone number, or do you know where he lives?"

She frowned. "Now what did I do with that number?" She turned and rifled through a pile of papers on the end table by the sofa. "It's around here somewhere."

"I need to ask him something about the case," I explained.

"Can you believe they still haven't found who did it? Honestly, on *Law and Order* they would have solved it by now. I don't think I'll get a good night's sleep until they do."

"Do you still think it was the man you saw?"

"Of course, it was. He looked guilty as hell. I tell you, find him and you've got the killer."

"You haven't seen him again, have you?"

"Thank goodness, no." She pushed her glasses up on her nose and scowled at the pile of papers. "Maybe . . . Yes, here it is. I found it." She pounced on a scrap of paper.

I saved the number on my phone.

"Thanks," I said. "I really appreciate this."

"If there's anything else I can do . . ."

"You've already been a big help," I assured her.

"Would you like a chocolate chip cookie? I just baked them this morning."

Before I could answer, she ducked into her kitchen and came back with a plate of cookies. When I left five minutes later, I had a small bag of them in my hand.

"How'd you get this number?" Kevin demanded.

"Barb Peterson gave it to me. Have you found out anything more about who might have killed Mr. Malinsky?"

"Stop. Don't say another word. It's not safe to talk on the phone. How about we meet at Starbucks at the mall?"

"No, not Starbucks." I didn't want to run into Matt.

"Then where?"

"How about Rounders?" Rounders was a popular bar near the university.

"Okay. How about seven?"

"All right. I'll be there."

When I arrived, he was sitting in a corner booth where he could see everyone who entered. He was wearing dark glasses, which only made him more conspicuous. I made my way between tables and joined him. The bar was crowded, mainly with university students.

"So why did you want to meet?" he asked. His eyes swept around the room nervously, checking out the other customers. Some were watching a soccer game on the TV mounted above the bar. Others were engaged in conversations over their beers or scrolling on their phones.

"I wanted to ask you a question," I said.

"What?" He looked uneasy.

"First, I want to apologize."

"For what?"

"For not believing your theory about aliens."

He stopped looking around the room and looked at me. "What changed your mind?"

"I think I met one."

He stared at me, then burst into a grin. "Yes. I knew it!"

"But that's not what I came to talk about. I have a question for you. About Mr. Malinsky's death."

"What about it?"

"If the feds didn't kill him, who did?"

"It had to be the feds. Barb saw him—the guy who did it. Didn't she tell you?"

"Yes, but I don't think the man she saw was a fed. So what else could he be? And please don't say an alien."

Kevin frowned. "Your boyfriend's a cop, right? Did he say it wasn't a fed?"

"No, and this has nothing to do with him."

"You're not going to repeat anything I say, are you?"

"Look, do you or do you not know what he might be if he's not a fed?"

"Well, he could be part of a shadowy organization— something with government ties but super secretive—a black ops sort of thing . . . maybe private funding."

It sounded like the sort of wacky idea a conspiracy buff would come up with. But I had dismissed his alien theory the last time we met, only to be proved wrong. Before I had come, I had promised myself to keep an open mind when I talked to him.

"Is there an organization like that?" I asked doubtfully.

"Sure. Two that I know of."

I didn't pursue that. "So you think the police might never catch the man who killed Mr. Malinsky?"

He shrugged. "Even if the killer was a fed, they might cover it up. In any case, I still think it had something to do with aliens."

Maybe it did. I suspected Mr. Malinsky had been killed because of the box and the star map. That was the only explanation that made sense.

"You might be right."

He grinned again, no doubt pleased to have someone agree with him.

As I drove home I thought about Kevin's theory about a secret organization. Whether it was a secret organization or a branch of the government, I knew sooner or later the man in black would turn up. If Kevin was right about who he was, there might not be much I could do to protect myself. At least I had gotten rid of the box. I just hoped he didn't find it.

CHAPTER 27

On Saturday I went to visit my grandfather's grave for the first time since his funeral. I took along a small bouquet of iris, his favorite flower. The cemetery seemed peaceful and lovely, stray red and yellow leaves fallen on the grass.

So much had happened in the month since his funeral. I hoped he would forgive me for having given away my mother's box. I thought he would if he knew just how dangerous it turned out to be. I couldn't help wondering what my grandfather would have thought if he had known that the box opened a portal to another world. He had always believed there was life out there in the universe. Little had he known how close he was to it—Kathleen, his daughter-in-law. She had kept her secret well. I wondered if my father knew. Did she tell him? And if she didn't, did he guess? Surely he would have questioned her sudden mysterious appearance in his life. He was an intelligent man, an astronomer who had spent years of his life gazing at the stars. He must have known, or guessed. And if he knew about Kathleen, did he also know about the box? Had he ever opened it? Or did he heed her warning that it was dangerous? Maybe he planned to open it someday in the future, a future which never came because of the car crash that cut short his life. And maybe if he had lived, he would have told me about my mother and the box.

I worried now that I should have found a different way to get rid of it. Apparently it acted as a beacon by emitting some sort of signal. Perhaps the signal was much stronger when the box was opened, but I suspected it was there even when the box was closed. Maybe when it was in the bank vault, the signal was blocked. I remembered how uneasy I felt that day when I carried the box out of the bank. Had I sensed the signal it was giving off without knowing what it was?

I wondered what my grandfather would have thought if he had known my mother was an alien. I'm sure it wouldn't have changed his affection for her. He had been a good man. He and my grandmother had done their best to raise me after my father died, and when my grandmother died from cancer, he took on the responsibility of raising me alone. He was always there for me. He encouraged me to apply to Juilliard and went with me for my audition and interview. I felt I owed it to him to carry through on our plan for my future.

I laid the bouquet of iris on my grandfather's grave. It seemed like such a small gesture. I wished I could give him more.

He would have liked Matt. It was unfortunate that it hadn't worked out between us. My fault. I had sabotaged our relationship. Now I would never know what might have been if I hadn't gotten scared and broken it off.

I missed my grandfather. What I wouldn't have given to go to his apartment and find him there working on his book, *A*

Guide to the Stars. Just one more time to tell him I loved him. One more time to hear his voice.

Sunday afternoon I drove to Sunnyside Manor to keep my promise to Mr. Merrick. I found him in a room of elderly patients playing bingo. One of the aides went into the room to let him know I was there while I waited outside. I wasn't sure I should interrupt him, but as soon as she told him I was there, he was ready to quit the bingo game. The aide wheeled him out in his wheelchair, and we all three headed down a tiled hallway toward the solarium.

I played the Beethoven sonata for him that I had been working on for weeks. I couldn't ever imagine tiring of it. It was a part of me now—coursing through my fingertips, muscles, blood, brain, and heart. The sound of my violin filled the solarium like the music from my mother's box had filled the hotel room that night in Sedona when I lifted off the lid. The sunlight slanted in, and I looked out at the red and gold trees and the flash of blue water in the distance where the lake was.

When I finished, Mr. Merrick had tears in his eyes. He reached out his hand and I took it.

"That was beautiful," he said. "You remind me so much of your mother."

As I drove home afterward, I still felt buoyed by the Beethoven. I could hear it in my mind as I turned onto University Drive. But when I pulled up to the curb outside my apartment house, the music died away. There stood the white SUV just a few car lengths ahead. The man in black had found me. Either he was waiting behind those tinted windows or he was already inside my apartment. I sat for a few minutes debating what to do. I could drive away, but that would just delay our confrontation. He would show up somewhere else later—on campus or at a concert or at the mall. I could not avoid him forever. Even if I dialed 911, I doubted the police could shield me from him. I might as well face him now and get it over with.

Picking up my violin case, I headed for the door to my apartment on the first floor of the old white house. As I had feared, it was unlocked. I nudged the door open with the toe of my shoe and tried to calm the pounding of my heart. Setting down my violin case, I looked around. The apartment was just as I had left it. My father's boxes looked undisturbed. At least the man in black hadn't trashed my apartment searching for my mother's box.

"I know you're here," I said. "You might as well come out."

For a long minute nothing, just silence. Then he stepped out of the shadows of my bedroom. Black suit, white shirt, tie. To my relief, he wasn't holding a gun or a knife, but I had no doubt he could produce a weapon in the flick of an eye.

He was the same man who had glared at me through the windshield of my car that rainy night I went to the library to finish my paper. The same man I had seen checking in at the desk in the hotel lobby in Sedona. There was no mistaking that look of cold scorn.

"If you're after the box, I don't have it," I said, thinking it best to let him know that right away. I didn't want to get my throat cut if I could avoid it.

"Where is it?" His voice was menacing. Just the way he held himself showed he was confident he would get what he wanted, that he felt in control. But I was close to the door. I could make a dash for it or scream if I had to. I had deliberately left the door open.

"I left it in Sedona."

He sneered. "You expect me to believe that?"

"Yes. You have some way of tracking it, don't you?"

He didn't answer.

If he couldn't track it, then the Native American woman to whom I had given it had done a good job of hiding it. Silently I thanked her.

"Where is it?" he demanded again.

"I gave it back." I had no qualms about lying to him. I had thought long and hard about what I would say if I found myself in this situation.

He glared at me. "What do you mean? Who did you give it to?"

"He said his name was Val." Doubtless Val was light years away by now. The man in black couldn't touch him.

He frowned. "What do you know about that box?"

"It's like a music box with moving lights."

He turned this over in his mind. "Where did it come from? How did it get here?"

"I don't know." I held my gaze steady on his, knowing my life might depend on whether he believed me or not.

"Are you telling the truth? Because if you're not—" The threat hovered in the air between us.

"Who are you?" I asked, emboldened by the fact that he hadn't attacked me yet.

"You don't need to know. If you're smart, you'll forget you ever saw me—or that box. But if you're lying, I'll be back."

I moved away from the door, giving him a wide berth as he left. For a few minutes I just stood there, my heart pounding, half expecting him to come back. Then I curled up on the sofa, hugging a small orange pillow to my chest. I hoped he would never find the box. I regretted now that I hadn't given it back to Val. He could have taken it back where it came from. I wondered if I was safe now. Apparently the man in black and his cohorts didn't know about my mother. And that meant they didn't know about me.

CHAPTER 28

I had three missed calls on my phone from Aunt Nora, who had tried to reach me while my phone wasn't working. She had not left a message, so I didn't know if anything was wrong. I thought of my poor great-aunt lying in bed with her broken hip. Suppose she had tried to get up and taken a fall? What if a new health problem had cropped up? I blamed myself for not having kept in touch with her since our last phone call. After repeatedly trying to reach her now that I had my phone back, I finally got through later that evening after my encounter with the man in black.

"Where have you been?" she demanded. "Why didn't you answer your phone?"

"Where have *I* been?" I said. "I've tried to phone you half a dozen times."

"Well, I've been busy. I met this nice man—"

"What about your hip?"

"I can't spend all my time in bed, now can I?"

"What man?"

"That's what I'm trying to tell you. He lives nearby, and we met while we were both out walking—"

"With a broken hip?"

"Well, of course not. There's a young woman who comes here and pushes me around." I assumed she meant in a wheelchair.

"I thought maybe you were having an emergency."

"No, nothing like that. But I was worried about you. I kept getting a message that your number was invalid."

"I was having trouble with my phone for a few days." I wouldn't mention my trip to Sedona. It would be too complicated to explain.

"Well, it's a relief to hear you're all right."

"So you have a boyfriend now?" I asked, amused. I tried to picture Aunt Nora with a boyfriend. She had been a widow for more than twenty years.

"Well, I wouldn't exactly call him a boyfriend, at least not yet."

"But you're okay?"

"Yes, yes. But what I called you about— Now what was it? Oh, yes. It was about your mother. I remembered something. It's not much, but I thought you might like to hear it."

"Of course."

"It was that time she and your father came to visit me right after they were married. She was looking at my books, and she had pulled out an old copy of *Alice in Wonderland* and was leafing through it. She said it was one of her favorite books. What she liked most about it she said was that Alice was willing to go down the rabbit hole even though she didn't know what was down there. At the time that didn't make a lot of sense to me. I always thought Alice would have done well to think a little harder before she followed that pesky rabbit down his hole. But now that I'm older, I begin to see what she meant."

I did too. Alice wasn't the only one who had been willing to go down a rabbit hole. I wondered when my mother had read the book. Was she rapidly trying to catch up and fit in? If it was right after her marriage to my father, and they had only known each other ten days before they married, she would still have been very new to our world. I saw how she might have identified with Alice.

"I'm sorry it's not more . . . ," my great-aunt said.

"Actually it's quite a lot. Thank you for telling me."

"Oh, I'm so glad you like that story. If I think of anything else, I'll let you know."

After the call ended, I sat there for a few minutes with my phone in my hand, thinking about what my great-aunt had told me. It was almost as if my mother had just spoken to me.

Although I had been back from Sedona for a week, I had heard nothing from Matt. And yet he must have known I was back. Joy or TJ would have told him. I could have gone to his apartment, but if one of his roommates answered the door, it would be awkward. What would I say? Besides, he had a new girlfriend now—the girl I had seen him with at Starbucks. Maybe he had no desire to see me or talk to me.

As I sat in class listening to Professor Thompson's lecture on Bach, my mind started to wander, and it occurred to me that even if I couldn't talk to Matt, I could talk to his mother. I was fairly certain she wouldn't slam the door in my face or make me feel embarrassed. I could explain what had happened between Matt and me, and she would understand. I very much wanted someone to understand.

But working up my courage to go see Matt's mother proved harder than I thought. What if she did blame me for what had happened? Matt was her son and naturally she would take his side. Maybe she wouldn't give me a chance to explain after all. Maybe I was no longer welcome in their house. And even if I was still welcome, it would be inconsiderate to show up while she was cooking dinner. Or during dinner. The minutes ticked by as I tried to work up my courage. It was dark before I finally climbed in my car and drove across the city to their house.

Ten-year-old Felicia answered the door. She broke into a smile when she saw me.

"Who is it?" her mother called in the background.

"It's Lauren." Felicia pushed the screen door open. "You want to come in?"

I hesitated. "Can you tell your mother I'd like to talk to her?"

I waited there on the porch, feeling nervous, wondering if it was going to be awkward to talk to Matt's mother. In a few minutes she stepped out of the house and joined me.

"Lauren! This is a surprise. Nothing wrong, I hope?"

"Do you have a minute to talk?" I asked.

"Sure. Let's sit on the swing."

It was what I was hoping she'd say. If we went inside, it would be hard to talk with the rest of the family around. The porch would afford us some privacy.

"Now what did you want to talk about?" she asked as the swing creaked and we swayed in a lazy rhythm.

On the way over I had rehearsed in my head what I wanted to say and how to begin.

"I suppose you know Matt and I broke up?"

"Yes, he did mention that."

"I think I owe you an explanation—"

She started to protest.

"Please. I'd feel better if I can explain."

"Wouldn't it be better to explain to Matt?" she said gently.

"I would, but I haven't seen him since I got back."

"Back?" She looked puzzled.

"From Arizona."

"I see."

I had a feeling she didn't. Maybe Matt hadn't told her I had gone away.

We watched a car drive past under the streetlight. Sitting side by side on the swing made it easier to talk than if I had to face her.

"It's a long story," I said. "I was hoping to find out information about my mother. And—" I wasn't sure I wanted to tell her about the man in black. Maybe better that she not know about him. Or Val. Or the box. I swallowed and tried again. "That night I came here for dinner . . ."

"Yes?"

"I thought Matt had the perfect family."

"We're hardly perfect. Stick around and you'll hear all the shouting and fights. Sometimes it's like a war zone."

"I don't have anything like that. When I go home, it's just me now. Even when it was my grandfather and me, it wasn't like that."

She patted my arm. "It's hard when you lose someone you care about. Give it time."

She didn't understand what I was trying to say. I wasn't making myself clear. I sighed and tried again. "I want to explain why I broke up with Matt."

"Honey, you don't have to explain anything to me. These things happen."

"But I want to explain."

A lone bicyclist rode by on the street. Somewhere a dog barked. Briefly the moon appeared from behind a cloud.

"I was afraid I couldn't give Matt a family like yours. And I don't think he'd be happy without it."

"Did you talk to him about this?"

"No. I thought of it as a choice I had to make between Matt and my violin. And I can't give up my violin. I don't think I could be happy without it."

"Did he ask you to give up your violin?"

"No. But if I go to Juilliard in the spring—" I didn't finish. The lump in my throat stopped me.

"I see. He would be here and you would be there. Not the easiest arrangement." She sighed.

"It doesn't really matter now," I said. "We broke up. But maybe you could explain to him. I hate it that I didn't get a chance to explain to him."

"Maybe you should call him."

I shook my head. "I think it's too late. I saw him at Starbucks with Sherry."

"Sherry?" She sounded surprised.

"Or some other girl."

"I doubt it was Sherry." She sighed again. "I don't know if he's got a girlfriend. He doesn't tell me everything. That's the thing about children. They grow up. You have to let them go."

"I told him we were too different."

"Did you? Lauren, let me tell you something. At your age the future is out there ahead of you. You can't know what it holds. Everything can depend on the tiniest coincidence. You turn a corner. You meet a stranger. Your life can change in the blink of an eye. Five minutes earlier or later you might not have met."

"Yes, but—"

"Life is messy. It isn't all planned out. You think right now that you can't have a family like ours because you haven't had it in the past. But how do you know you can't have it in the future? You think you have to choose between your love for Matt and your love of your violin—but maybe you don't. Maybe you can have them both. You don't know until you try."

The screen door squeaked and Felicia leaned out. "Mommy? Warren won't let me watch TV."

Her mother smiled. "Come here, baby."

Felicity darted over and squeezed into the small space between us. She snuggled against her mother, and her mother planted a kiss on the top of her head.

"I should go," I said, rising. "If you see Matt . . ."

"You should call him."

I did call—several times, in fact—but each time it went to voicemail, and I couldn't bring myself to leave a message. I didn't know what to say. He had a new girlfriend now. I had seen him with her. And no doubt that was why he didn't phone, or text, or turn up on my doorstep.

I told myself I should at least tell him about the man in black, but with each passing day it seemed less urgent. What exactly would I tell him? That the man in black had killed Mr. Malinsky? I had no evidence. And whose word were the police going to take—mine against someone who quite possibly worked for the government? Not likely. And anyway the man in black might not bother me anymore now that I didn't have the box. So I did my best to put him out of my mind and go about my routine of classes and violin practice. Meanwhile, I had a concert coming up at the end of the week to look forward to.

As Friday night neared, I felt a growing sense of anticipation. The world of the concert hall was what I lived for, what I was meant for, and where I felt most alive. That at least hadn't changed.

From the minute I entered the auditorium that night, I felt my pulse quicken. Excitement was in the air. Other musicians were arriving, setting up their sheet music, tuning their instruments. I was tuning my violin when Sheila arrived, looking elegant with her hair upswept and tiny earrings glinting in her ear lobes.

"You missed rehearsal," she said by way of greeting.

"I had to go away for a few days."

She raised an eyebrow inquiringly. "Did it have anything to do with the boyfriend?"

"I needed some time to think."

"So are you good now?"

"I think I am."

She smiled. "That's all that matters."

I smiled back. I would miss Sheila when I transferred to Juilliard. She was like the big sister I had never had.

There was no more time to talk. We both had to finish tuning our violins and set up our music.

When I was satisfied with the sound of my violin, I took several deep breaths to calm my pre-performance jitters, just as Mr. Hajek had coached me to do. His words drifted through my mind like a mantra. I must put everything else out of my mind and focus on the music. I must be ready when the time came to start, ready for the conductor's signal.

"Look," Sheila said in a low voice.

With her eyes and a lift of her chin she indicated the audience. Puzzled, I followed her gaze. Matt was coming down the aisle. He was wearing a white shirt and a jacket I hadn't seen before. He didn't look up as he made his way to a seat. Why was he there?

I took more deep breaths. No time to think about it now. It would have to wait. I had to be ready when the moment came to reach for that first note.

As on that other night, he was waiting for me afterward just outside the door. A half-smile played on his lips; his eyes were warm. Other concertgoers lingered, chatting, but I saw only him.

"I heard you went to Arizona," he said.

"That's right. I did."

"Did you find out anything about your mother?"

"Yes." More than he could possibly imagine.

"My mother said you came over to the house."

"Matt—"

"She said you saw me with Joanne."

"That was your sister?"

He smiled. "Want to go somewhere for coffee or a bite to eat?"

For a split second the world stopped turning on its axis. I had looked forward to this moment for days, afraid it would never happen. And now here he was. And here I was. Had I just turned a corner?

"I'd love to."

ABOUT THE AUTHOR

DEANNA MADDEN has taught literature and creative writing at colleges on the U.S. mainland and in Hawaii. Her publications include short stories, essays on literature, the novella *The Haunted Garden*, and the novels *Helena Landless*, *Gaslight and Fog*, *The Wall*, *Forbidden Places*, and *The World Beyond: A Novel of Ancient Greece*. She lives with her family in Honolulu, where she is at work on her next novel.

www.ingramcontent.com/pod-product-compliance
Lightning Source LLC
Chambersburg PA
CBHW022017170626
46808CB00001B/451